# INTO THE QUIET BARREN

## JON H. EDDY

INTO THE QUIET BARREN

Cover art & design by Alex Helmintoller

First print edition, 2025

ISBN: 979-8-9919892-1-3

www.jonheddy.com

*Dedicated to A. Tomaszewski*

# PROLOGUE

IN THE SUN COUNTRY, the bullet holes in the walls of school hallways and classrooms, three and four feet from the floor, had always been patched, but the effectiveness of the concealing became dependent on a painter's ability to match color. And since good tradesmen were hard to find, the evidence of little broken bodies glowed.

It was hot there in the Sun Country. It felt as if the sun was always up and blazing through a thin atmosphere, starving the amber waves of grain and drinking up even the swamps and sewers. The sun was so powerful that it burned off the old names, too. City names. The names for people. Naturally then the renaming became a great source of conflict. This was how the everwar re-formed, continued. Coast to coast and ear to ear, new posses mounted.

And the domestic supply of infants bloomed, right on time, pushing a current of unprotected children into two main tributaries. Those who were sweet on new technics pooled and eddied in the big cities, the Numeral strongholds, and slid in packs, animated by a cloud-based vigilance, armed with panes of glass, these tricky mobiles with cameras and connectivity, patrolling the streets for anyone whose energy was suspect.

In the smaller haunts, where Theocrats asserted their influence, the little ones collected small-caliber firearms and learned to shoot back, so the staccato rhythm of twenty-twos and little nines punctuated the low valleys, the mountains and the flatlands. Tinny reports, there and gone again with little echo, gave the rural landscape a deadpan affect.

On the outskirts of midsize cities, ground troops mustered and took what they could by living out the fantasy of former wars. Digging trenches and rolling barbed wire across the steppes, moving in slow columns, harassed by drones and autonomous crop-dusters repurposed with harder chemicals. Wine country burned, either by torch or electrical malfunction.

The people who had the proper means left the Sun Country, went upward, in planes, to other countries, or higher up in towers, finding homes amidst the heavy nimbus. And the delicate filaments inside those who stayed on the ground snapped under the weight of so much loss and the charge of so much fury. Where belief and knowing failed them, a portal opened to the deep. Around it grew new machines. The people in Gracehaven, in Three Notches, in Mirror Bay, in Little Apple and Grand Portion; we found the business of leaving accessible then, via inward routes, passages winding down, into cooler regions, into the evernight, where there was no moon, no stars, no sun to guide us, and no one trying to kill us, to string us up and hang us blue.

And here, far away on the outskirts of nowhere, our low-pile city stretched. The rhythmic, repeating impacts of the factory and the dull buzzing of the refinery floated on the wan draft. A hundred million lights. This gleaming invention. And here, where our bodies were safe from spurious detonations, we had another enemy. The night itself. Any darkness.

# ONE

ON BEACON STREET and across the city proper the night song came from speakers, mounted in the eaves, the upper-story windows and rooftops, not every one, not every building, for materials were harshly rationed, but enough to blanket the rough sleepers and day-shift vagabonds lilting through the town with the recording of heavy industry, of squeaking brakes, the voices and happy shouts of a thriving, peopled city, and behind this the roaring engines of airplanes, a deft reminder of the war above.

Here, in the Third District, the five and six-story buildings had brick facades and little space between them. Lit foyers, arched-over, with smooth tile steps, and Sun Country mailboxes for decoration. Printed trees had been planted at intervals along the sidewalks, the trunks wrapped and canopies of painted green leaves strung with delicate light bulbs, shedding loose points of light onto the pavement, where the falling ash gathered and December Valence waited for the car.

On the streets of Pluto City, a woman could walk through its darkest sections, any time during the long and constant night, and feel bodily safe. This was good. This was promised. But she had accepted Malor's offer of a car, and so she waited.

The invitation had come as a surprise. She wondered at how long it had been since she had seen him. The passage of time was hard to measure in Pluto City. There was summer and there was winter—heavy embers and chunks of metal and of bodies fell from the evernight sky in the summer; ash and bits of paper trickled lightly from the pitch sky in the winter—but without a sun or moon to chart the days, only the night song repeating the sound of industry for working hours and the sounds of bygone nature for the time of rest, the days bled into one another. Even the newspaper she worked for didn't put dates on their issues; they just rolled them out each day with new stories and advertisements. All she knew was that it had been some time since their last conversation, when their relationship had ended, it must be years ago now.

So when the car landed, as a swan might, and lifted its wing for her to enter the cabin, she did so with a mix of trepidation and curiosity. Why, after all this time, had Malor beckoned? The inside was plushly sewn with leather. She recognized the driver. Malor's assistant, Gist.

"Long time," he said, as the car lifted gently into the night. "How've you been?"

"Indeed it has," said December, and left it at that, preferring to gaze out of the window and let her mind relax.

Pluto City had at times a certain vacant quality. It was wider than it was tall, with the occasional high-rise to dispel the myth that it really wasn't a city at all. For all the buildings that December flicked past as the car maneuvered inland, toward the center of the city, there wasn't anybody walking on the streets. She bisected Hope, which ran through the very middle of the city, and was capped on one end by the central library and on the other by the central hospital, where she and Malor had first met.

On her first night in town, once she had taken up the new body, he just so happened to be idling out front of the hospital in his black Magnum, a car which even then had impressed her. Malor had been a friend at first. A sort of chaperone. He played an instrumental role in her forgetting of the old world, the cruel world, seeding her with the big story, the one that held us all, eventually teaching her the sensory limits and capacity of her new body.

She had gone to school and lived in the library along with the other new charges, where she would attend classes every night, taught by the matrons, who were more like teachers, more like mother-figures then. They taught the value of believing in the light and removed any alliances we had held to the Sun Country, dissolving the Theocrat and Numeral leanings, replacing it with a philosophy of consumption. We learned the history of Pluto City, what foods defined us, the civic character we were to uphold. The city's founders, we called them lumens, were benevolent. They had only wished to give us a chance of a fresh start, free from worry, and so trained the critical and faithful natures out of us, to prepare us for our work.

December wondered idly at where her classmates had gone. Why hadn't they kept in touch? Each of the students had their own dormitory built into the basement of the library, right there on Hope Street. For the first stanza of her life here, Hope Street was her whole world. Born in the hospital and trafficked up the same street to its terminus, to the library, where she slept and ate and learned to love her new home. It was only with Malor that she ever saw anything outside that repetition, when he would pick her up in his car and take her on excursions, to see the rest of the Second and Third Districts and stop for short layovers at his apartment.

But eventually they'd ended and she had reorganized herself around that fact and now, here she was, sitting in his car once more, floating to the racetrack to see him drive, having no idea why he had sent the invitation.

At Olympic and $7^{th}$, the buildings opened up and gave a view of the high-rises in the Second District, and toward the outskirts of the city, the great wall, rising to protect us from the encroaching darkness of the evernight. It all looked so real.

Soon, she was between two taller buildings, the vision gone. Street lamps rose at intervals, dropping cones of orange hue onto the sidewalk, defiant against the evernight. A crooked middle-finger to the end, each and every building, where no one ever came to shoot you while you slept. She rolled the window down and took in the night song, now approaching early evening, evidenced by the ebbing-away of barking dogs and honking horns and the rise of cicadas' hum. The sound of wind through trees, the city breathing out, the end of day.

However many people really lived here, Pluto City was their refuge. An improbable outpost, hidden away from the hot war above, the sort that obliterated wicker homes and had neighbors killing neighbors. Great tanks, treading over highways, moving town to town, piloted by the Numerals or the Priests, it didn't really matter after a hundred or maybe a thousand years of breathy carnage. Here, you were safe. Didn't matter if you worked the lab or the market or slept on the street with nothing more than a threadbare bedsheet to call your home, there was food to eat, and nobody strung you up and hung you blue. December knew this. She knew

the big story. She remembered it often, carrying this impreg-
nable sense of safety. She was happy now. Had grown
happy since her end with Malor. And yet, she felt an ache.

THE RACETRACK CAME INTO VIEW. A thousand
lights, threaded along a circuit, made from a long stretch of
8$^{th}$ Avenue, which at the end of the straight curved into a
big, looping, and then a smaller coiling turn through King
and Vestige, and then into another long stretch of 12$^{th}$
Avenue, where the engines would scream, echoing off the
buildings, and then jagging into a tight little chicane, then a
long left-hander that came and came, before petering into a
weighty pit straight, back on 8$^{th}$. December could hear the
engines warming up before her coach had even touched
down.

Motor racing wasn't the city's most popular sport but it
kept a lot of people very busy. Mostly the princes and the
makers and the mechanics and their friends. Those who
formed their personalities in the war above, who had retired
from the fighting, only understood themselves within the
context of violent dynamics, and so retained the taste for
spectacles that occasionally caused catastrophic injury.
They needed something they could take seriously, around
which they could build important lives, of the sort that
allowed them to claim a certain *joie de vivre*, a certain prac-
ticed irreverence.

Pluto City was perfect for that, for this empty risk, for
this glory without consequence. Here, you could build all
the toys you wanted, make them as gnarled and as beautiful
as you like, and you could make them loud. You could make
them roaring and powerful, and you could make them go

fast. And you didn't really have to pay for anything because the resources didn't have any cost. Which isn't to say that building cars and winning races was easy. The founders had cast over the sport a consistent sort of physics that rewarded certain designs over others. Engineering prowess within these guidelines was a premium good. Yes, it was hard work, but the raw materials were abundant. You just had to take them. The people had already been paid for. You just had to feed them. You just had to leave out a little bowl of milk.

December understood this. She had no qualms about her role. The city was in the business of purpose and protection. She was in the business of imposing its relevance. She hung around the confluences of money, electricity and blood, shaping the splatter into products, into reasons for living, for winning, and for the celebration of immortality. In a word, she was a writer. This city was the only game in town and her employers needed it to stay that way. You couldn't have people wandering off in the dark, or gathering up the means to really remake the place, or punching out to try their luck in the Sun Country. A city is a sad place without any people. Without any people, a city just dies, becomes a memory and then an absence, an empty field somewhere in the fog. This was a particularly distasteful outcome to the people who had built the city. The lumens. Those who laid claim to such a title. The princes, the makers, the mechanics, and their friends. Her job was to make them real.

The car touched down and the door opened softly. She could hear them. A crowd of onlookers had paid their joules for entry and gathered in the stands that had been erected at certain entertaining straights and corners. Normal people, sucking down imitation lager and whooping at the night. On December's side of the fence, she didn't need a ticket, didn't need a badge. The right people recognized who she was, and so she stepped out of the warm embrace of the floating car and made her way to the paddock club.

In here, it was bright, too. The lights were many and of a high, blue-tinged wattage, presiding over the rich buffet and the many starched white shirts and bright yellow shirts, and shirts of bright crimson, and orange, and of neon pink. Steel carafes of coffee and the faux-porcelain plates, traveling by creamy palm, matched the smiles and matched the cutlery. This was a room where you spoke of nothing and imagined money.

December loved it here. She liked the effect it had on her skin, the way it neutralized her little cracks and insecurities. These were her people. This is where she belonged. Amongst the lumens, amongst their light. She had to admit to herself, it felt good to be back.

She helped herself to a thin flute of sparkling wine, standing with its platoon on the starched white table cloth, and turned to watch the room, and then she saw him. Moving buoyantly, surrounded by a gaggle of very serious adults, asking seriously for him to sign little objects with their felt-tipped pens.

Malor Pendegast was dressed for the race. He was a driver, so he had on a fire-proof suit, zipped down at the waist, exposing the body's fine musculature. He had one of the good ones. Tailor-made, strong in places, soft inside. December knew his contours. She savored the slender, uncomplicated moment that viewing an old flame proffered, before the burn scars inside of her tightened, and their eyes met.

He moved through the crowd toward her, sloughing them off with a combination of long strides and delicate rebukes. She found, quite immediately, that she wasn't ready to see him, that it hadn't been long enough, and that suddenly she was back in the old feelings of resentment she had felt when he had ended their tenure together.

"Hello, Ember. Fancy seeing you here."

"You invited me."

He shrugged and smiled. He had those little dimples and a strong jaw that was clean-shaven, but in the eyes there was always a darkness, a little shadowy absence.

"Well, I hope you know I don't take it for granted that you came," he said. "It isn't every day I see a friend."

"Who says we're friends? I'm just here for the spectacle."

"Then I certainly hope we can deliver."

"You do have it in you to fall short."

Malor's face changed, dropped away into something else for an instant, then rose again in a playful smile.

"How's the catalog?" he asked. Even when they had been together, he liked to tease her about her work.

"The paper's good, same as ever," letting his comment slide off of her.

"How's the family," she said.

When they had been close, they would only ever roll around in secret. Stories of their laughter never reached the echelons of his mother's or his father's ears. She was the progeny of a worker bee, a technician. This was an unavoidable fact which Malor had allowed to form the limit of their relations. And it was quite a shame, by December's estimation. Malor was lonesome in his own way. The only son of the city's founder, even in rarefied circles he breathed different air. With her he had been happy, had stolen pieces of the golden sun, here where for him there was only cold need. And she knew he knew this. She could see it in the way he had carried himself when he was with her. Felt the way he became lighter, unencumbered. But alas, when given the choice between delighting in his own heart and silencing the love in him, he chose the latter, out of a fear and respect for his father. On this, December had no effect.

She let the heavy knot that hung in the air between them grow, pull them to it, pull them down, and sipped her beverage, waiting for him to tell her why he'd actually invited her.

"You know," he said, finally, breaking the little spell that had transfixed him, "there is something I wanted to talk to you about."

He motioned for her to follow him to one of the tables, in a slice of quiet, away from the crowd. December sat across from him, pretending to let bygones. He looked around. Took a certain caution into his voice.

"Before you start," she said, holding up a hand. "I didn't come here for editorial advice. I'm just here to watch a race and eat whatever snacks they put out."

"Of course. I never tell you what to do. Only what's in your interest. And I'll just say, without a doubt, this is more important than whatever it is you're working on. I promise you. It's a good scoop, and deadly important to your readership."

"Why does it feel like you're trying to sell me dirty underwear?"

"Look, this is me talking to you. Not my family. Not my dad. There is something really wrong with the city. The city is unwell. I believe our time is running out, and the people ought to know about it. Maybe there is a solution hiding amongst the workers. The engineers and builders are fresh out. They are exhausted. They tell me it's only a matter of time until the power goes, and if that's true, the people here should have a chance to get their affairs in order, and burn down what they can."

"Are you okay?" she asked. He sounded hoarse and, despite his bluster, desperate.

"Quite frankly, I'm mad," he said, and leaned forward. "For too long these people have worked their tails off. The least the lumens could do is have the decency to let them know the dream is done. And I want to give them the truth, give them the honesty they deserve, and I think you can help me do that."

"People are always talking about the end of the world, the end of the city. I usually chalk it up to boredom. But you. Haven't you got enough to keep you interested?"

"This is serious."

"Sure sounds like it. What's your angle?"

"Well, my hope is that when we wake up from this, they'll remember me. They'll remember who was real with them, and who they can trust."

"And you want me... to help you engender trust?"

"Who knows me better?"

"That's what I'm saying."

"Look, I'll be honest with you. I'm reinventing myself, and I could use your help. I can't tell you all I know, but things in the city are about to change. I'm qualified to know."

"And the role I play in this vision of yours is, what, your publicist?"

"You're more than that, December. You always have been. The change I'm putting myself at the center of, well, it's big."

"Certainly seems that way. Big as can be, and lucky me in the middle of it. I should be fawning."

"The old rule, the one that has held us, is dying, and in

its place something else will rise. I hope I don't sound too cocky saying it, but it's time for me to take up my father's mantle. It's too heavy for him now. And yes that makes me powerful, but only so far. You can help me, and I can help you. You can't be satisfied writing ads for the rest of your days here. I know you want more."

"Historically, what I want has never been a real concern of yours. I have the evidence to support."

"You're right to say that's how it seemed. But of course I cared. I just felt trapped. And now I don't. Now I can see the prize. A new life. With you in it. I don't feel so itchy now, or if I do it doesn't bother me like it used to, because I'm about to shed this skin, and wear a new day, and in that day, I can see us, Ember. The life you wanted, the life we wanted."

There was a time when such words would have melted her, but she was past frozen to them. Now she could only chuckle at him, a thin, rocky laugh.

"You're broke as hell. Same as always," she said.

"What was that?"

"I don't buy your little pitch. And I don't appreciate being lied to."

"I promise you, what I'm saying is true."

"You haven't told me anything. You haven't said a single thing. I know your song, same as always, pussy-footing around, trying to get me to bite or I don't know, get all invested in half a wish. So you can use me, use up my energy."

"There it is again. Your favorite story. No one's trying to use you. It's not using you if you benefit. You are not a tool, December. You're more than that. I wish you could see that. Wish you could get over that little low class *thing* of yours. It's why you people never make anything. You can't get over this false rift in you, the fake little scars that you still listen to, that tell you that you were never worth anything."

"No, Malor, that's you talking. That's your voice."

"All I'm asking is for you to cover the race tonight and write a profile. If you pitch it the way I say, I'll make sure your editor accepts it."

December pretended to consider it, buying some time as she let the agitation in her drop away. She wouldn't let him see her getting shaky.

"Am I a ghost to you, December? Was I nothing?"

"We haven't seen each other for two, three years, and you come at me asking for a favor. You can't blame me for not champing at the bit."

"This is important, the most important thing anyone could be working on. Trust me, you'll see."

"No, Malor. I'm really not interested. I'm happy now. Happy with my work and with myself."

"Nobody's happy with themselves."

"Speak for yourself," said December.

She stood and walked away, happy to have gotten under his veneer. She had been right to shut him down. She felt fine about it. After all these years. How long did they go back? To the beginning, right? To the very beginning, and after all that time, he had the audacity to treat her like his little automation.

The indignation burned off quickly, leaving in its place the same ache that had been with her all night, or maybe ever since she'd been here. The sort of bad feeling you get used to, that takes another feeling, with its own acreage, to distract you for a while, and then return to, and feel it stronger, like it was the first time.

DECEMBER WAS STILL interested to see the race. She found a spot in the box above Malor's team garage, which was open to the sounds of the twenty engines revving up. From here she could see the pit straight, a long section of 8$^{th}$ Avenue, lined on either side by high fencing, and lit completely by two rows of tall, powerful lamps. Across from where she stood, the tall faux-brick and stone buildings, the panes in their windows glistening in the evernight.

She knew it was all synthetic. Everything that she could see was ported in, run on servers. People always said that it could happen. The idea of it was central to the city's culture. Of course the lights could go. That's why everybody worked so hard to keep them on. This work against the dark united them. Their common enemy was everywhere, which meant each citizen of Pluto City was surrounded by their friends. That was a part of the big story, the big book, from which all of the pages that she wrote were torn. But truly end?

No, if it were true, she would have found out somewhere else. She would have seen some sign, some observable fluctuation in the power. Or there would have been an official announcement. The automations of their government, which doled out resources, would have begun to ration the energy supply. All of this around her took energy to print. If they were hurting, she would know. These lights would not all be strung here. There'd be no race.

And you had to consider the source. Like many sons of great men, the role given Malor left him little room to improvise. He had always been developing alternates of himself. Little personas. He enjoyed intoxicants. Anything that totaled up in his blood as an escape. The garbled phoenix story that he told her could have just as easily been a wish as a rendering of anything extant.

December felt the particles of the deck beneath her feet vibrate with the revving engines and leaned over the banister and looked into the pit lane. The cars were shiny, long and low, with pointed snouts and bellies hugging close to the ground like predators in the night. They crept lazily out of the garages and gathered up a great roar then as the pack of them tore into the track. She gazed at the spectators gathered in the stands, all of them happy and exuberant. What a wonder this city was.

She slid her eyes up the tall buildings across the street. The broad sides of them that had moments ago been grids of windows morphed into singular, glassy panes. Infinitesimal pixels reorganized into great screens, showing a montage of other places along the track, broadcasting an expert coverage of the cars as they maneuvered through the twists and turns, warming up for the race. It was a tight track, populated by slow turns that poured into the high-speed sections.

December couldn't help but find Malor's car. Number twenty-seven, a white car, clean of advertisements, trundling around the final turn and settling into its grid spot. Ahead, the long pit straight, four cars wide, ran down into a fast decision, where the road narrowed and was able only to fit two cars across, before turning sharply into an abrupt, u-shaped turn. After the warmup lap was completed, the cars sat and vibrated. She could feel them, waiting for the strobe, then with a roar, they were off.

The fifth and sixth place cars were slow at the start and allowed the seventh place car to slip between them. The seventh-place driver got excited. He missed his braking point, carried his speed into the corner, and locked the front brakes. The car slid but the driver caught it and, though losing all his speed, made the corner and joined the fray, having lost four places. Miraculously, there was no incident.

As the race developed, the cars through the back and midfield became evenly spaced, and carried out a neat concertina effect at each turn, all slowing, and grouping in the slow corners, before accelerating out and spreading once more.

December looked around her at the faces of the people cheering in the crowd, or just standing there, blissed out, letting the growling, screaming engines echoing off the buildings subsume their thinking. She felt calm. It was good here. It was good to be safe.

The crowd oohed and December's eyes found the correct screen as Malor and the other two cars at the front of the pack came around the last corner.

Malor had taken second. Ahead of him on the straight now was the purple number eight car. But just barely. Number eight took the inside line. The shortest path in the run down to turn one. Malor, on the outside, taking a slightly wider line had better grip. On account of this, eight's lead diminished. The two cars zipped past, running at two-hundred, as Malor feinted left, the tiniest little flick, before churning out of the slipstream and onto number eight's right side.

Malor was a nose ahead entering the braking zone for the fierce kink. His car was on the inside of the corner and he braked late, later than the number eight car, and so as each car began to rotate, number eight's front wheels were level with Malor's back axle, and in one stiff movement, eight turned in hard, and swung into Malor's wheels.

The effect was instant.

The back end of Malor's car, light from all the force

gathered in the front of the car, swung. His wheels lost all traction and all of his speed and his force flew sideways.

In the blink of an eye, the car tipped and slammed the top of Malor's helmet into the hard cement wall. The impact destroyed him, crushing his body down into the thimble of a cockpit, tearing the car into broken threads of faux carbon and remembered steel. The sound was massive. The race was stopped.

As the emergency response vehicles played their part and scraped up the remains of the body and of the machine, putting them in separate piles, the people in the crowd cheered. Filled with mirth, they toasted one another and laughed and drained their cups of imitation lager. This is what they'd come to see, this reenactment of carnage, reminding them of their comfort here in Pluto City and of the safety they enjoyed. December knew the story, and wasn't she happy in it? Shouldn't she be cheering also?

Instead a sickened feeling rose from someplace deep in her. She left before the race restarted.

# TWO

DECEMBER STEPPED INTO THE CITY. The ash fell
lightly. Just tiny, floating bits of burnt paper, so small you
could make out only fragments of the words they held. She
didn't need an umbrella. She didn't need anything. She'd
walk home.

As she walked, she thought of Malor. What an actor.
What a child. It wasn't the first time she'd seen him die.
They'd revise and rebuild his body. No expense was spared
for a body's repair. It was part of the deal here in Pluto City,
this scorn of death, this celebration of immortality. Such
that the violence she had seen carried for her very little
meaning. She was sure he'd get his story, whether she wrote
it or not. The story would gather steam and he'd be cele-
brated for his bravery and commitment to the fight, as if
there had been any risk at all, as if his preservation had not,
since his rebirth here, been guaranteed. And who knew
what he'd come back as. Maybe there was a plan, just like
he'd said.

She hated being pulled into his story, yet again. This
was the cadence of their relations. He was gone from her,

and her life was mostly placid, and then suddenly he'd fall into her like a rough stone into a still harbor and she was moving in his ripple until she settled.

Eventually, with the benefit of hindsight, she would come back to her understanding that he had really only been a disturbance. But seeing him up close always reminded her of old pains, collapsing the cool pleasure of distance, pulling her right back into the waters she felt she had just climbed out of, convinced once more that what they'd had was truly special. She felt what wasn't, she felt bereft, like she was missing something crucial, as though without it, she would never be complete.

She remembered their first trip through the city, riding in the passenger seat of the nicest car she'd ever been in, feeling the furthest she ever had from home, yet free, burgeoning, on the cusp of a fresh life, as he pointed out the stories in the architecture of the homes on Ford and the secret pubs on Master, the particularity of the orange street lights merging with a warmth that flickered in her new chest. This, before she knew any of it on her own, and now everywhere she looked was soaked with him.

Why was this? Why was she so easily pulled into these waters? It made her feel contingent, as though she had been built not to contain her own echoes, her own life, but the lives of others. She supposed it made her good at her job. She could disappear into her subjects, and this mostly provided her with a deep satisfaction. In fact, it's what she lived for. The pursuit of understanding them gave her a soft and introspective way of understanding herself. But tonight it felt as though perhaps there was no her. She felt grainy and inconsequential. As though she herself was a figment, an illusion. This was the ache.

She shook her head, as if to toss out her thinking by

centrifugal force. She craved beauty, and charted a detour. December knew the city now. Could grasp anything she wanted.

December walked through the arts district. The street was crowded. Music thumped from a four-story walkup, propagandists and dancers spilling onto the sidewalk like pretty daddy long legs.

At the corner of Hope and Stupor, a mural took up the whole side of the Banquet Building, a tall, airy cube of imitation railroad steel and clean glass, with one flat cement wall holding it all in place. The wall was painted to give the effect of cracking, of great chunks coming away at the middle. Between the cracks, blue sky, and as the eye moved the sky opened wide and there, just above you, was the nose of a falling bombshell. The painting was so good that it made you want to run and made you understand that it was too late to move.

———

THE FLOWER MARKET was open year round and occupied a grand courtyard in the open space between four squat brick buildings. Anchored into the sides of these buildings, one corner each, were strong, tensile steel lines that held a protective sheet over the flower stalls, catching the fallen ash, bits of paper and shrapnel. An array of fixtures gripped the piping of a metal grid and poured even streams of light onto the flower stalls below, where buckets of long-stemmed paper flowers rose from deep plastic pots and flats of smaller blooms crouched together on cooking trays, stacked for viewing. Scent of jasmine, rich and sweet and the sharp, citrusy hue of rose seeped from olfactory speakers at the corner of each stall, reminding potential customers of the Sun Country, where flowers used to grow, where maybe they still did. Here, the workers left the hoods of their coveralls unzipped, heads lifting like stamen from the folds of dark canvas that gathered around their shoulders as they performed the movements of trimming and primping and unloading the freshly made origami from white vans.

December stood on the outskirts and watched these repetitions. This time of night, it was mostly just the workers, chatting at the end of day, perusing the stalls, which were arranged on either side of a central walkway that wound around the protective tenting's central beam, always wet with the running water that for a moment you imagined had been used to keep the plants alive. She breathed in the memory of rich, Sun Country air, put her hands behind her back and strolled, one foot in front of the other.

Each stall specialized in a different sort of offering. There were flats of small, delicate pink and white blooms. Then the taller, almost silver stems, curlicued by spearlike leaves and thin, almost iridescent, deep indigo petals that drooped like wagging tongues.

Looking at the flowers, these reproductions of what she'd left behind, she asked herself: do you think they still bloom in the Sun Country? Was there any of it left? There had to be, she thought. And what of the war? Was the war still on? This was one subject the paper never covered with any detail, as though it was forbidden.

The story went, that was the old world. The dead world. Why bother yourself with ghost attachments? This home, the new home, was the only one that mattered. Which was not overtly stated, but bled through the lines that even she wrote. Now, she wondered, stronger than usual, what was it like now on the surface? Was it spring?

Did the morning dew still gather in droplets on the delicate shoots of new grass? How long had she been here? And hadn't she always planned to return? This sojourn of hers was never intended to be permanent. The thought of it roused an anxious energy in her. She was buzzing now, a bit off kilter.

When December felt this way, she liked arrangements that were dark and moody. Deep blues and purples, and maybe a single white or yellow bloom for contrast. On such nights, an arrangement too bright felt like an affront. She found what she was looking for in the stall numbered fifty-eight, where a thin, weathered man stooped over a bucket, pretending to trim at the edges of a bundle with a pair of rusted clippers. He was missing two fingers on his clipping hand and dust crowded the fissures of the wrinkles that rippled through his neck and up into his cheeks and forehead. When he looked up at December, his eyes were bright.

And the image would stay with her.

As she filled a bucket with purple and blue, all of the lights in the market browned low, the wattage struggling to circulate, before dropping away into a deep and total darkness. A breathless swath of time passed, wherein the gravity that seemed to hold every particle of every flower and the floor itself, the trickling water, and the bodies of the people, left them for the silence of eternal absence, on which the nature of our demons and their principles are formed. And then the deep, groaning buzz came as the power returned and the infinitesimal particles found again the shape of living and December stood looking at the bucket in her hands, and at the protective sheet above her.

"What was that?" December said.

The elder man, who had returned to his clipping,

though now with a coiled intensity, stopped for a moment. She could tell he heard her. Then he shook his head, as though to clear her from his memory. He wouldn't look at her. And around her the people returned to their habits. When confronted with a steep and imponderable cliff, what choice did you have but to carry on as you had before?

December paid and left the market clutching the bucket of flowers with both arms. As she paused on the corner, a street-sweeping carriage ground past her, picking up the fresh detritus. She stole a glance Downland, down the hallway formed by the buildings on either side of Limit Street, toward the very edge of the city. This far Down, in this corner of the city, the evernight was close. December could see where the great wall rose, protecting us. She shivered, and realized the carriage was long gone.

# THREE

DECEMBER'S APARTMENT had come to feel like an outpost. Improbable. Precarious.

It consisted of three rooms. One for sleeping, one for eating, one for writing. A utilitarian outpost in which she had installed herself, alternating between these three rooms, in very much the same order over the two full nights that had passed since the outage. She had left it only twice, each time to walk the two blocks to the corner market for food and for a copy of the *Pluto City Sun*. Back in her apartment, in the writing room, she read each issue front to back, looking for some mention of the outage. She found nothing. Of course, Malor's accident was covered liberally. Her editor, Heather Mercy, had two bylines. The first, a play-by-play of the race; the second, a follow-up piece suggesting the possibility of a full recovery, attached to an advertisement for the Body Shop.

But there was nothing about the outage. Nothing about any city-wide catastrophe of any sort. No ebbing resource. No problems really at all. Unless you considered the closure of a sandwich shop on 5th some kind of tragedy. December didn't. She had been on one occasion, and the material inconsistencies of the faux deli meats, she agreed, warranted the consequence. Yes, it was as though the outage hadn't happened.

Meanwhile, she had received a new assignment. This time, for the FoodBox 4000. Attached to the content brief, which was rather short—Heather's prose was always terse— was a full-page image of the subject. A lovely device with rounded corners, a door which one could pull open to retrieve the generation, and a grid of numbered buttons, where entering certain codes would prompt the machine to make a desired dish. Porridge, bowl included, whole chicken, golden potatoes, frozen yogurt, rack of lamb, and so much more. No cleaning necessary, no need for any paste, all you needed to do was plug it into the wall and ensure your subscription was in good standing. A wonderful invention, the article for which December would normally be primed to write.

She began her process, putting the brief aside and focusing on the image. She let her eyes graze peacefully on the small details of the machine, as though it was her own face in the mirror, gradually associating the physical details of the FoodBox 4000 with her own visage. But it didn't work. December was far too aware that she was staring at a printout of a sort of microwave. And this had much to do, she realized, with the outage. What meaning did the abundance of instant sustenance have if what it took to create its masterpieces was, quite possibly, running out? What did it mean for her and everyone she knew? Did the power failure she had witnessed, that she had felt with every pixel of her, amount to a total threat to their existence here?

In the big story, there was much talk about the possible end to their world, but there was an antidote built in—that this refuge was permanent, the energy that powered it limitless. The lights could never actually go out. That was fairytale. A conjured threat that people in her line of work trotted out to give their articles more weight, to keep the trains on time and the people working. If the lights really could go out, well that was a different story, and not one she understood.

However the more she typed, letting her mind loosen, trying this and that path into the new story, she found herself able to embody her subject. She, too, felt the capacity from within to conjure vast couplings of proteins, fats, and sugars. With every sentence that she typed, she felt more solid, whatever emptiness she had felt from seeing Malor ebbed away. But each time she left her desk for a snack, or a cup of tea, or to gaze out of the window in her living room, she felt a panic creeping in, one of the sort that had no language yet, that she could not understand, but only feel, deep in her, a sister to her normal ache. And so she paced. She tried to read. She listened to the radio, hearing nothing that roused her. Just the usual dramas and bullet points. Production figures and population growth.

It occurred to her that she felt a sense of propriety over the city. In her past life, she had helped to build it in her own small way, working at the transfer station with her father in Mirror Bay. She could recall the lazy, tepid sea and the roiling mists that daily enveloped the little life they led together on the western edge of the Sun Country. Numeral land, far from the fighting, but steeped in its effects.

She had not thought of this for some time and could only sense the vague outlines of who she'd been, as if the mists prevailed over her memory of the place as well. Having arrived at the precipice, though, she wished to remember it more clearly, but encountered a wall inside

herself, demarcated by a Do Not Enter sign in bold lettering. She felt her sister aches sharpen and needle her.

December finished her article as an afterthought,
finding ultimately a passable arrangement of words that
incorporated the beauty and convenience of a truly special
object, owing all to the perfect safety and abundance of
their home, of Pluto City. She sent it off and she sat and,
without the work to distract her from what the work had
been about, stewed in the raw ingredients of her creeping
dread.

The image of the gardener returned to her. His weathered hands, his missing fingers, the rough lined, leathery
neck and the watery eyes, glistening in their almond
crevices, framed momentarily before the lights went out.
Had she known the man, before? Had he come through the
station? Had she transferred him? And there again, the
blockage, the limit of her inquiry into what had come
before, leaving her alone with the sharp ache, as though the
walls of her apartment were lined with knives, pointing
inward, closing in.

The panic grew in strength and overwhelmed her
quickly. Not the idle kind, easily stanched with thoughts of
grandeur—a pretty city view, pretty futures, or the piped-in
stories of imagined decadence. No, she had to leave, had to
move, if she ever meant to breathe again.

And now the street, walking. Neon lights in the shop
windows, selling toys. The sound of engines, the stamping
rhythm of the factory. The day song, sound of traffic and
honking horns. The day song, for the productive hours. She
couldn't breathe. Her lungs like little paper cups, fit to burst
from any intake.

December stopped at the intersection of Grand and 8th
and scanned the buildings. She needed something. A

matron. Yes, this might save her. She walked up $8^{th}$. She knew they had an office, four blocks up, and so she ran.

When she reached the six-story brick affair, the doorman clocked her need, and opened wide the door. A receptionist, a pretty automation, listened to her calls. Same-day meeting, something now. Nodded head. Took her hand, depositing her on the third floor. The cheap carpet, hard and gritty underfoot. And now the office. Warmer light. The matron's voice, soothing, scratchy, distant. December collapsed onto a couch.

━━

MATRONS MOVED QUIETLY. Just a swish of the robes, which were deep red, beginning in a deep hood and flowing downward over narrow shoulders, large bosom, wider hips, and stopping just short of the floor. Matrons had no feet. They merely floated. The face was made of a kind of creamy porcelain, the expression constant. The eyes, narrow caves, deep and eyeless. The mouth, frozen into a slight, impassive smile, opened a little. It did not move when they spoke and the voice came as though from a gramophone, with the clicks and pops of an old record, echoing slightly, as if playing from the other side of a long, dark hallway.

You would see them sometimes, walking on the streets in the night, speaking to no one, smiling always. It was hard to figure how many there were. They had offices across the city. Though imperfect in their delivery, they supplied a needed service for those in the city who felt suddenly and imponderably alone. No matter what time it was, you could get a meeting, and no matter which you met with, they each could access any conversation you'd had with another.

December had sat with a few of them over the years, never able to tell them apart, never feeling completely healed, but calmer. Able to walk out of the office a little lighter than she had been feeling when she walked in. Better able to return to the demands of the city and its work against the night.

Once she had gotten the concept of her breathing to level out, she sat up on the couch, across from the matron who sat on a little stool. The window beside them showed a plain view of a few buildings. The room was quiet, as though the window to the city was just a painting, as though they were far far away from anything else. A little capsule, full of calm.

"Tell me, child. What happened?"

"I don't know. All of a sudden I couldn't breathe," December said, and laughed quickly, like a chirp. "As if I have actual lungs. It's all so stupid."

"It isn't stupid. Clearly you were feeling something big, and it took up all of you."

"That is what it felt like."

"Having a panic is a common response to reaching the precipice of something you don't understand. There's opportunity for that in every night. It's a wonder it doesn't happen more."

"Yeah, well I guess this one felt different."

December could hear, faintly, from somewhere in the robe, the matron's body hiss and moan as it recalibrated.

"Tell me. What were you thinking about when the panic happened?"

December felt the brief impulse to leave, but quieted it. She wanted to be here. She needed to talk, and so she did.

"I was at the flower market after the race. The power went out. It didn't go out for long, but it went totally out.

I've never seen it before, and it scared me, and then I was reading through the paper and nobody talked about it. There was nothing, and I got to feeling like maybe it hadn't happened. But I could remember it."

"Of course it happened. It happens at the beginning of every winter."

"I don't remember that ever happening before."

"Maybe in past years you were sleeping. It's a slight fluctuation in power as we switch over to winter reserves."

December had no evidence to offer up for the occurrence. Only the memory of a deep absence, the impression that it gave her, and the image of the gardener. His shiny eyes, and the way he hadn't responded when she spoke to him. As if she hadn't been there at all. Or maybe it was that once the transaction was completed he did not want her to be there.

"The outage alone is nothing to be afraid of," the matron went on. "But what is important is why it scared you."

"Well, I had seen an ex before it happened. That didn't feel great."

The matron processed, quickly.

"Was it Esme or Malor you saw?"

"Malor."

"Did you two speak?"

"Yes. He told me the world was ending, and then at the flower market the lights went out."

"And was that all you talked about?" said the matron.

December noticed, vaguely, the sharpness that came into the matron's voice, but went on. You had to play the game to get any relief out of these things.

"It was the only thing we talked about that had any substance," she said. "There was a little banter. I was already a little angry just seeing him. It always happens this way with him. Just when I've gotten around to forgetting him, there he is, and I'm back in the same old waters."

"It sounds to me like this is the origin of your panic."

"You know, I've thought a little about it, and I don't think that's it. He's a finger in the eye, pointing at something, but not the thing itself."

"Very good. So it isn't the ex and it isn't the outage. Do you have any idea about what the issue might be?"

"I don't know. There's just this ache. I guess I just feel guilty all the time. Like a little embarrassed and ashamed."

"That is an intense mixture of emotions to be carrying around with you," said the matron in the softest voice she had at her disposal.

"Yes," December said.

"But they are emotions, which means you can change them. Do you have any guess as to what's really causing this?"

"See, I don't know. It's just a feeling. I don't have any words for it. I just feel certain it's why I'm alone. Why I stay that way. Why all I do is work. And it's not about Malor. I know that. The ache was there before him. It's there all the time. It's just been especially loud these past few nights. The outage made it worse."

"I see," said the matron. "And why do you think that is?"

"If I knew that I probably wouldn't be here."

The matron processed. A new record was placed on the gramophone. The voice took on a slightly different tenor. The voice that came was deeper.

"December, I wonder if you'll allow me to suggest something. It may cause you a little pain, but you'll be safe. I promise."

"What kind of pain?"

"I'm wondering if you'll take me with you into what you felt in the dark, when the world disappeared for you, and you were floating."

The impulse to leave that December had earlier felt came back more strongly now, and this time she heeded its caution. The energy in the room, she could tell, had shifted. The calmness the matron channeled had become pregnant with something else, which December knew was there but could not touch.

"I appreciate you asking so gently, but no. There's nothing there to go to."

"Of course," said the matron. "What I'm having trouble understanding is what you could possibly have to be afraid of. In this city you're the safest you could be."

And it was as though the words that came out of December next were pulled from her. She felt them leaving her, as if through quickening fingers.

"But what if the city is all there is? What if there's no returning? No home to go to? I'm afraid it's all gone. That all we have left is synthetic. That I'm surrounded by nothing but lies, and that I am one of them. Just an utterance."

The matron processed. She noted this, and underlined it.

"How long have you been feeling this way?"

"I don't remember not feeling this way."

"Since before you came here, then?"

"Yes. I mean I think so. For as long as I can remember."

The matron processed. And when she spoke again it was as if another record had been put on the gramophone.

"What you're feeling has very little to do with the city.

This sense of responsibility you feel isn't from here. It was born elsewhere. You carried it with you."

"Why can't I let it go?"

"You might need it."

"Why? It hurts me. It doesn't do anything good for me."

"But maybe it does. Maybe you are responsible for something terrible. Maybe that's the truth you're looking for."

"Okay," December was caught off guard, hurt, and in that pain began returning to herself. "What am I supposed to do with that?"

"I suggest you look inward first for who to blame. Reach into your wellspring and sift for the reasons for why you are guilty. You'll know them when you find them."

December laughed, fuller this time. She felt an anger rising. Beneath the poetry of the matron's voice, she heard a pointed sort of hunger, impersonal and roving.

"And how does one do that, exactly?"

"It happens to be a service I provide. I can help you, if you'd like."

"Of course it is. No. Thank you. You've already been so helpful," said December, acidly.

The matron was silent for a long moment, its eyeless face giving nothing.

"Very good. Will that be all?"

"Yeah. I think it will," and she was already standing and moving for the door.

When December returned to her apartment, the kitchen was dark. She found the bulb in the ceiling had gone out.

# FOUR

THE LIGHT HOUSE occupied the entire second story of a squat stucco building in the Third District, floating, in a way, above a block of storefronts that had either been long abandoned or never occupied in the first place, their stiff glass fronts silty with age, the empty foyers swallowing what light they could. For a moment, December allowed herself to marvel at the detail in the coding.

Inside, the radio was playing. She knew that voice. Esme's. It was one of her radio dramas. The one about the vampire, flying over the city spires, watching us below. Can't you sometimes hear the flap of wings? December had been with her during rehearsals. The scratchy playback ricocheted off the low ceilings and down into the tight maze of shelves, barely wide enough to contain her shoulders.

Szewski sold a vast array of fixtures, wiring, bulbs, and all the tiny pieces required to build them and hang them. What pieces weren't stuffed in thick, open-top cardboard boxes or lying naked on the shelves, he hung, and lit. The smell of dust and ozone from the burning filaments gave the place a warm and earthy hum. However, as December navigated her way to the back of the shop, where Szewski stood, always, bent over his workbench, which doubled as his register, magnifying loupe pinched over his good eye, performing some inscrutable surgery with his big gnarled fingers and delicate tools, she noticed that about half the bulbs on the show pieces were out. Shadow crept, thickened, and with it the quiet muttering of night itself.

Szewski was already shaking his big, pale head as December hurried around the last corner toward the workbench. She had always preferred the older apartments, which from time to time needed improvements, so she and Szewski were familiar with each other, and the exchange of honest feelings sometimes found its place.

"It's very bad, December. Very very bad."

Usually, Szewski was jovial. A tall man, with an elderly body, robust but for the crooked leg, seemingly at peace with his place in the world. He set down his tools and grunted as he stood.

"My lights, all of them. It is as if they don't have enough to eat," he said.

"I'm having the same problem. I counted four dead bulbs before coming over here. I was thinking you sold me a bad batch."

December winked to let the old man know she was kidding. Szewski, despite his murky tidings, showed his boyish grin and quickly tousled what remained of his wispy hair.

"Ah, yes. You know I was always quite the swindler."

"Tell me," said December. "This is why your store is so gloomy?"

"Look at them," he said, sweeping his arm over his holdings, "half of them won't even go."

"Do you think there's a problem with the wiring?"

Szewski shrugged the great hocks of meat that were his shoulders.

"Likely, no. Not if you are having the same problem. They need a certain wattage. Short of that and their filaments cool. I've had people coming to me all day putting it on the bulbs. Angry, most of them. One man, I won't tell you his name, who has been coming to me for twenty winters, broke a bottle on my step and threatened me with the shard."

Having breathed this into the room, Szewski seemed to shrink a little, grow weary.

"I always sell the very best," he said. "You know that."

"I know that," said December. "Besides, I already used my bottle on the bread guy. Tried to sell me a loaf full of holes."

Szewski attempted a smile.

"Do you know what's causing it?" December said.

Szewski raised his shoulders theatrically. "Why should I know? Of course nobody says a thing. Where are our leaders? Where are the voices that tell us that they're going to fix it, that I'll be okay?"

December thought of her conversation with Malor Pendegast, someone close to it, in a position to know, and how wholly unsatisfactory his rendition had been.

"I've been struggling with it, too," she said. "The way I understand myself, who I have understood myself to be. I'm confused about what it matters if, really after all, these lights of ours are going out. My—you know, I think I've said this before. I understand myself to be a writer, but I realize more and more that I don't know what that means. I guess what I'm feeling is the power seems to be going out in the idea I had of myself, like I imagine the bulbs here going out feels for you."

"Yes," Szewski mustered.

December put her hand on the back of his.

"What's wrong?" said December.

"I have been thinking of my wife," said Szewski. "Which for me is an occupation I prefer to avoid."

This was the first time he had mentioned to December that he was, or had been, married.

"Your memories," ventured December. "They're coming back?"

"Yes, yes," said Szewski.

And then he told her.

In the Sun Country, he had been living in a small town, ten or so miles from the factory where he worked. A beautiful drive, he said, along a quiet two-lane strip of highway with deep meadows on either side and a rich pine forest, scenting the air year round. A detachment of soldiers, boys really, had set up a checkpoint on that quiet highway between his home and his work. He had driven the road every day for twelve years, but never a day beyond this one. They tortured him. Pulling him out of the vehicle first and knocking the butt of a rifle into his skull once, then twice. When he was drowsy they held his foot upright beneath a back tire and rolled over it slowly and had threatened to do the other if he didn't tell them where his daughter went to school. He passed out instead of telling them and when he woke up he was alone with the verdant fields, waving sharply in a cold wind, the dying sun, and the suffocating pain in the bottom of his leg. His wallet was gone. His car was gone. He crawled home and his home was gone. The house stood, yes, just as the body that had contained his wife remained.

Szewski finished the story in the quiet, wide-eyed submission of a man, decades later, still gripped.

"And I don't know why, but I can't stop thinking about the way she used to talk to the spiders who made their webs in the shower. She would try and coax them out of the way of the water. She was scared of spiders, but she would carry on these conversations, attempting to guide them as a friend might, or sometimes pleading with them not to crawl toward her. I would lay back in bed and feel so in love with this silly woman. Lately I have been thinking only of this, this music of her bargaining with the spiders in the shower and asking myself again and again, what was the value of a world that would kill her? It is why I left it, to come here, to a new place, that yes was not so dangerous, but most importantly for me did not contain the clues for what I'd left behind. This was the agreement that I had with Pluto City. This was the bargain that I made, and I feel as though, if the city fails, I will be left with only what I sought to put behind me."

"I fear that, too," said December.

"You have also been remembering?" Szewski said.

"Whenever I reach back and try to grasp anything that happened from before, I come up empty, but I can feel it waiting for me. Almost whispering."

"What does it say to you?"

"That it's all my fault," said December.

"I can't help feeling the same," said Szewski.

"What happened to your daughter?"

"I do not know. I never found her."


DECEMBER DID NOT REMEMBER WALKING home. All she knew was she was crying. She sat on her couch, free of shadow, and felt the words of Szewski's story as close to her as breathing, replaying for her like an autonomic response. His answer to her final question cut her deeply.

*I do not know. I never found her.*

She had not been found either. There had been no finding. Forget a mother—she never knew her—but where was August? Why had he let her go off into the world without him? From Gracehaven to Mirror Bay, they travelled. She, always at his side. His assistant. He, the one she always wanted to make proud. He had been her only constant, her only friend.

Why had he abandoned her? Or was it she who had abandoned him?

She sunk into an impression that the reason she was so alone was the even doing of her own hand. That of course, if she had worth, she would have a father and she would have a love—but instead, no, it was all because of her that she was lonely, because it was all because of her that she was worthless. Little trash goddess, little trash girl. Easy come easy go, just throw away. You never found her because there wasn't any reason to go hunting for a candy wrapper once you'd eaten what's inside.

And when the memory came, it devoured her.

---

SHE COULD SMELL THE SEA. An onshore wind carried the scent of the red tide into the bay and through the bony docks, where trawlers and sailboats tipped gently in the harbor, and between the small cracks allowed by the aging door jambs and window sills, depositing tiny particles of the musk onto flat surfaces in every house, and every shop along the intersecting streets of a modest downtown, and up, still, to the golden rolling, razor-wired hills that over-looked Mirror Bay.

In a big house, on Chief Street, the air flowing through the vents into the rich cedar rooms was warm and quiet. December and August got ready for work. She must have been twelve then. Her shoulders and the set of her jaw told of a preternatural seriousness, etched into those who had been, by the luck of the draw, chosen to bear loss early in life and grow too fast. Later on in life she might have been funny, but such internal structures hadn't yet been built. So for the time being she carried all this tension in her shoulders and in her neck. It gave her headaches. It made her want to drown. She could remember the splitting heat as it gathered in the center of her brain, electrocuting her, and it would last for hours. For hours she couldn't see, and in the bright and dark undulating of her vision, amidst the tortured whomping in her skull, she imagined diving into a cold, black sea, and ceasing to be in pain. This chapter of her life had been more or less defined by the coming and going of these storms. But on this day, she had been feeling mostly good.

The two met in the kitchen. August had thirty-five years to his name but the body was fresher. He'd taken one of the new rigs, one of the prototypes. He didn't even have to pay. The mechanical wonder was a gift to him, courtesy of his employer. He wore the University pin on his outer coat and carried a briefcase. December had on her new scarf, a stark red chambray, just as they had ordered.

"Are you ready," August said. The voice was a lot like his old one.

December inspected the contents of her satchel. In the short time that they had lived in Mirror Bay, she had acquired a black-spine book of fiction, a stopwatch, several pens, and a roll of twine. Satisfied, she zipped it closed and hoisted the leather strap over her shoulder.

Together they walked through the neighborhood, which had been built along the range of golden, rolling hills, that were sparse with gnarled oaks and cut lengthwise by a high wall, the boundary, that stretched on for a hundred miles in either direction.

The street was lined on both sides by houses that had once been colorfully painted. December had named them and she spoke to them. There was Pilar, with clay tiles for a roof and a stocky front door. Melvin had broken windows and a graying, overgrown yard. August walked behind her as she turned to each of them and nodded solemnly, as though she were leading a mighty procession. The roiling fog collected in tiny droplets on the arms of her wool coat and carried her messages seaward.

December and August left the neighborhood and came nearer the cliffside. When she held his hand, she could tell the bones were different, but she never said anything. She held it now, not for her comfort but for his. While he did not say it, she knew he was nervous. He was still getting used to this job. Out of the whorls of condensation came something motionless and heavy. A cubed boulder of grainy cement. Tall, with big windows aiming out to the sea. The natatorium.

The boy was waiting for them out front. He was a little older than December. Small for his age. His right arm stopped short at the wrist. He'd lost a hand. The bandage was fresh and already needed changing. August took a warmth into his voice and greeted him.

"I heard you can help people get away," the boy, whose name was Milo, said. He held up the pamphlet with his good hand.

"Why don't you come in, and we can talk," said August.

A light rain had begun to fall. The water ran in thin trails down the natatorium's great window, obscuring its view of the bay, where the sea churned and slung little fists of sea foam. Inside, it smelled faintly of chlorine, even though the old competition pool had for some time been empty. December watched Milo's eyes trace the long cables that ran across the decking, from a blinking green generator in the distant corner of the grand room, to the pool and into it, where they plugged into the machine, which had been installed atop the dry, gritty tiles of the deep end.

"Is that it?" Milo asked.

"Well, young man, that depends on what you're looking for," said August.

December had by then grown accustomed to August's play. The early part of any conversation with a potential client was spent on understanding which pitch to give them. To the faithful, he was a shepherd, listening for the bell that hung from round the neck of the sheep who had been lost from its flock. He spoke to them of rebirth, of the chosen path, and of the providence that awaited them.

To the coldly rational, he was a tactician. He spoke of calculation and the gifts of shrewdness that his clients possessed, had earned and developed, and brought to bear by choosing to come here and take control of a life that had heretofore been suspended amidst the war. What had been robbed from them, their agency, was here now for the taking. Their algorithms had been interrupted and this machine would make it right.

"It says here you can set me up with a new life," said Milo, who had gotten the pamphlet open but left a little smear of rusty crimson on the lettering. The pictures showed the plush cabin of a ship, a grand city, full of sunlight, "but all I see is that thing."

Milo jutted his chin toward the machine. It stood about eight feet tall and had a squat bearing. The front of it had knobs and dials, a little square convex screen, two circular tanks, side by side, that were empty now, except for the paddle wheels inside. A clear hose ran from the machine to a holster on the side of a chair, which was mostly metal, and had straps for the arm rests and the headrest and an opening in the back so you could access the neck.

"Tell me. What is it you like best, young sir?" said August, improvising.

Milo looked up at August. December could tell he was measuring him.

"My dad used to tell me stories about sailing the open sea. I always wanted to do that, go out there and live on the edge of the world, always moving, seeing everything there was to see."

"It sounds to me like you want to live a life of adventure," said August, "and the war's gone and messed all that up."

"Pretty much," said Milo, "and this doesn't help." He held up the stump of his right wrist.

"What if I told you that was still possible?"

August clicked open the clasps on his briefcase and the sound echoed sharply. He came out with high definition photos of open-concept homes, and sporting venues, and clean, ample restaurants where happy people gathered.

"We set you up with a whole new life," said August. "Where you're safe to pursue the opportunities that were taken from you here. In our city, nobody's after you, no one can touch you. You'd have everything you lost."

Milo winced and glanced toward the door.

"What if I don't like it?" Milo asked.

"You can always come back. It's likely the war won't last forever, and in the event there is anything left worth coming home to, you'll have a place, in a body just like mine that requires less upkeep and feeding than yours does now," and August came close to him, and peeled back a swatch of tissue on his forearm, exposing the gears and steel bones and fine strings of composite material, "the city here, your new home, will be a refuge. You'll be safe, you'll have work—but not too hard—and you'll be able to pursue the life you should have had here, that was robbed from you."

This was the pitch that December had heard him say, a hundred times, when they had moved through Gracehaven, door to door. There, the racket of gunfire and small artillery was constant. The people there required less convincing. Here, she could tell, August was running out of things to say.

"I don't know," said Milo, and now he was looking again at the machine. "I thought it would be different."

Each of them in that room had lost their world, the world they knew, the world that felt, for all its recognizable flaws, like a home. December understood this as much as anyone. Maybe more than most. All she'd known was the tumult of a changing tide. She'd grown up in it. She was not so much made for it as she was made from it; chaos was at the very foundation of her blooming person.

"Have you ever had a dream," she spoke up, "where you feel like you're someone else? The kind of dream where you are a different person, in another world, all its own, and when you wake it feels far, far away, but also like you can feel it inside of you, like it was true."

Milo looked at her and he nodded.

"It's like that. All it is is staying in the dream, where you're safe and where you're brand new."

"Have you been there?" he asked.

"I have been," she lied. "And you've been there, too. You've already had to give up your home in place of something new, a place you didn't recognize. The only difference is that in the city, no one's trying to hurt you, to take away all that's good."

And Milo believed her. When he looked at her he saw a girl who had woken up one morning in a new life and had to figure out a way through. Her voice was tempered with it. That much was true.

"Does it hurt?" he asked.

"Just a little, but you've handled worse," she said, looking at his stump wrist.

"Okay," he said.

"Okay," said August. "December, would you mind?"

Of course, they had their choreography. She went across the room, her footsteps echoing scratchily. In a shadowy corner, away from the influence of the wide and dripping windows, was the power supply. A staunch cylinder with green diodes on the front. She switched the power regulator, and for a moment wished it didn't work.

August led the way to the pool and climbed down the ladder into the shallow end. He helped December and Milo where their legs couldn't reach the bottom.

"Be careful," he said as they walked toward the machine, down into the deep end. "The tiles are slippery."

When Milo reached the chair, he rested his hand on the head rest, absently, while his eyes rolled over the particularities of the machine.

"How's it work?" Milo said.

"Think of it this way," said August. "This machine here

may not look like much, but it does one thing very well. That is, it's able to exist in two places at once. The machine here in Mirror Bay and the machine there in the city is really just the same machine, aware of its position in both places, and when you sit down here, think of it like you're settling into a chair over there, too. All you have to do is lay back and close your eyes, and when you open them once more, you'll wake up in your new home."

"But if I'm sitting here, who's sitting over there? Whose body?"

"Well, yours. You—the important part, what's inside—is just shifting over, laying claim to a life that's already yours."

"And my new body," Milo asked. "It'll have both hands?"

A warmth came into August's voice.

"I'm sure of it," he said.

The chair creaked as Milo sat into it. August nodded, to himself as much as his passenger. December watched all this. She had been listening, like a tree might, digesting sounds and feelings with her roots.

"Isn't there anybody here you want to say goodbye to?" she asked

It was as though they could not hear her, as though she had not spoken.

"What's the city called?" said Milo.

"Pluto City," August said.

Milo tried out the syllables on his lips.

August readied a syringe with a golden-colored serum and made Milo comfortable by injecting into the meat of his shoulder.

As the serum ran its course through his bloodstream, Milo stole one more glance toward the natatorium's open door, and then he was out.

"Are you ready?" August said to December.

She nodded before climbing up a small ladder that had been positioned on the backside of the machine. From the flat top of the machine, she could reach the important buttons.

August adjusted the neck rest so that the opening in the back lined up with the space between the fifth and sixth vertebrae. He needed to think precisely now.

August lifted the hose from the hook where it hung, unsheathing its long, tensile needle. Thousands of tiny, gleaming fibers lay flat along its surface. He focused the sharp point on the downy tissue between the two knuckles of the cervical spine, and made a puncture, and pushed the needle down, and steadily down. He closed his eyes for this, and allowed the feeling in his hands to guide him as he buried the needle to its hilt. A second, smaller needle, he fed into a smaller run, upward, into the base of the skull.

And with the body attached to the machine, August concerned himself with the second portion. There were coordinates at the bottom of the back page of the pamphlet. He hadn't memorized them yet. He entered them into a keypad, and a corresponding graphic blinked onto the little monitor, like a deck of paint swatches, fanning out. A cursor fixed onto the edge of a red-hued swatch.

He looked up to December, and nodded, and she engaged the correct sequence of buttons and switches. Once she got the machine going, and the needles performed their function, the tiny hairs lifting, it was said, to withdraw data packets from the nervous system, the hoses filled with colored liquid. Each person had a hue. Milo's was iridescent purple. The machine began to hum and the liquid of his essence flowed into one of the circular tanks and the paddles turned. The machine whirred and digested and the body continued to be still. December felt the back of her neck cool and tingle. Wind lashed the windows with the water it contained. Outside, the sea thundered.

AS EVENING CAME, the storm cleared and August and December piloted their small vessel out of the harbor. The body, wrapped in a bedsheet, lay on the deck.

"Excellent work today," said August. And she saw his pride, and she felt it swell in her, too. She had been helpful, and that was good. The sun dipped into the horizon, leaving the last of its brilliance for the seagulls to consider.

They trawled into the deeper water, past the mile buoy. August killed the engine and with his strong body hoisted the empty one over the edge and dumped it in the water for the sharks or anything else that was hungry to consume.

December watched as the current took the body under and she wished that she could pull Milo back into the boat and take him home with her, and wake him, and have a friend. But Milo was gone now. She watched the body sink, deeper and deeper, the white sheet reflecting the last of the day, just a vague shape now, before it disappeared and left her alone with the beckoning deep.

# FIVE

DECEMBER WAS wide awake when the day song's opening salvo fell across the city, the clatter of a railcar and a moaning whistle, announcing to its citizens the beginning of a new day. She was nauseous, her center of gravity compromised, reeling from the memory of Milo and the lie that coaxed him into coming here. How many more had she and August transferred?

She recalled the pamphlet that she and her father had used at the Mirror Bay and Gracehaven transfer stations, that had been distributed across the Sun Country during the war. The pages were glossy, the pictures showed pristine beaches, summer cottages butted up against the lapping waves, and neighborhoods built amongst the trees, the architecture seeming to sprout naturally from the land itself. The words printed on the folded pages told of a brand new world, free of the violent competition for resources that plagued our species in its corporeal domain. What she saw before her now was like a city built inside a windowless room with the door locked and the little light we had flickering out. The disparity between the narrative that sent us here and the reality we inherited was stark. And December had been a part of it. Maybe she still was.

She attempted to take pleasure in the arrangement of purple and blue and yellow flowers, but it felt to her as though the particles had been rearranged. Their shape and coloring was the same as she remembered them to be, but they carried another message on their petals, not of beauty, but of candy wrappers, thrown away, left in the street to be stepped on.

The bulb from Szewski's shop, newly installed, performed as it had been designed and cast light onto the corners and surfaces of December's kitchen, where she stood now, reading over the new batch of assignments from her editor. As she had come to expect, ever since the power in the city had begun to ebb in places, there was no mention of the outages there or in the paper writ large. The omission felt more grievous now after the return of Milo's memory, and after her conversation with Szewski, which had illustrated a dire need for answers amongst the city's people. The content briefs she held now, printed on the cheap, wispy paper made the part in her that stood for a stomach turn.

Heather Mercy's language in the briefs was cold, as usual:

*Just in time for winter: umbrella sale. Boots. Machetes. We need to impress upon the reader that the boots are of the highest quality and durability, with deep treads and thick soles. The machetes are perfect for tending to the most riotous of gardens. The umbrellas are the same as usual. Most people already have them, as you know. Spruce them up a bit. Two-hundred words each. Due by the quitting horn, tomorrow night.*

And, as expected, on each of the three pages contained

behind the brief was an image of the subject. A pair of ankle-high, imitation-leather boots. A nearly-steel blade with cushioned handle. The usual bat-wing-black umbrella. Each product was unremarkable in and of itself. But there was something about them that struck her as absurd. What did any of this matter if the lights were going out? Her interpretation of her role in the city, as an imposer of relevance, as a storyteller, felt all of a sudden wrong.

December gripped the thin pages as though they might steady her, crinkling them as she sat into the chair at her desk, carrying out the muscle memory of her work. This rote process, feeding paper into the machine and typing out the opening lines of her prescribed task, as though she herself was an automation. But the words that came had nothing to do with flashlights, boots, or garden tools. She couldn't focus on them, couldn't force herself into the perspective of a boot.

She wondered, what would happen if she didn't write them?

December understood that her living arrangement was contingent on her employment. If she didn't make her deadlines, the paper, the catalog, whatever it was, would find someone else to carry them out and she would lose her dispensation of joules and this apartment. She would be a vagabond, living on the street until she found another job. She would still be fed, of course; she would not go hungry. This was a part of the deal, a part of the big story. So there would still be a life for her, and of course she could find other work. Not as a writer, for she'd have burned a bridge with the only publication in town, but at a restaurant maybe, taking orders, polishing the tabletops and drinking glasses and cutlery. Dignified work, one might say, free from the forced repetition of what increasingly felt like, not the big story, but the big lie.

December looked into her bedroom mirror. She was grateful for her body, grateful that it was free of the headaches that had plagued her in the Sun Country, that when she stepped into the night, no one sought to kill it. She commanded the body each day to wake, to see and feed itself with particles of energy, to work, to seek out the work of others that she admired, with these two hands, ministering the city's story through its objects.

She liked the perspective her work granted her and mostly enjoyed the act of arranging letters in compelling order. It gave her a place to put her busy mind, an outlet with which she could organize her self, give her self some semblance of continuity, even if that meant empathizing with inanimate objects. The possibility still sung to her. The possibility that the work had meaning, or could.

She supposed that whomever at the paper determined the editorial regime might not be aware of the need in people to understand what was causing their lights, the city's life force, the bedrock of their refuge, to falter. Perhaps the way the *Sun* had operated before the outage was just fine, and now that the material circumstances of the city itself had changed, so too would the paper's function. She imagined that she could be a part of this, a driving force in a needed change.

She opened the window of her third-story apartment and looked out on the gleaming impossibility. Can you see it? A tiny island of light alone on the inky firmament, far from danger. The streets a patchwork of miracles. Each cobbled stone as precious as a last breath. The three and four and six story buildings, weaved and painted by blood and bone and lit by the song of every desert. Can you believe we have succeeded in bringing forth this refuge? It wasn't our choice to start the war, but it became our place to protect the unwanted and illegible that it caused. Recall how tenuous it all was and how important it is to take up your own fight against the ever-present, ever-choking advances of the darkness that surrounds you. The gleaming city, this improbable masterpiece of protection and prosperity needs you, and you, and you to do whatever you can to keep the night at bay.

This was the story as she had learned in school, that coursed within her. And she was proud, even now, to play her part. But to feel the guilt-tinged dread creep in, that really did belong to her, made it hard for her to breathe. She had built this city. Yet the capacity for pride was tarnished by the memory of her deception. Was this the city's chief ingredient? Was it hers? How many of the people walking now throughout the streets of Pluto City had she plied? There had been no sunlight here, and there was no angel waiting for her in the mirror, and the light by which she lived was going out.

She watched the street below her and counted the good things, totaling them up as a line of defense. On the street below, the pottery shop was opening for business. The purveyor himself moved back and forth on the sidewalk in front of his shop, sweeping the night's ash into the gutter, at home in his work instead of looking over his shoulder. She could see the alabaster plates on display. Thin units. If this were Gracehaven, each one would have been crushed. And a light traffic of personal vehicles moved in order, up and down the street. Bright ones, bland ones. Evidence of opportunity and selection. No explosions met them here. Hadn't she helped these people? Even if it had taken a little lie to ply them, their ultimate safety was worth it, no?

December felt the cool pinch and tingle on the back of her own neck and placed her hand on the smooth, simulated skin. She pressed her fingers into the soft indentation between her imitation vertebrae, felt the phantom pain of her own transfer. She had gone through it, too. And hadn't she benefited? Hadn't she traded a life freighted by the constant threat of bullets and nooses for one of safety and a chance of fulfillment?

The warm light from the new bulb cast an even glow onto the countertops and tile floor. She admired the walls of her apartment. The painting, vivid with color, that hung large on the wall before the low-back, almost-leather couch in her living room. The small, iridescent stones she kept on the hutch, beneath the hand-made, hand-painted terracotta lamp. All of this was hers. This body, this home.

And yet, she wondered, what became of Milo? Had he stretched into a life of comfort and influence, or of adventure, as he hoped? How had any of them fared? How would she know? She imagined going door to door, as she and August had done in Gracehaven, knocking on each, carrying not a pamphlet but a question—how's your life?

But where would she start? And how would she recognize them? Years had passed. It wasn't as though she was in the same body as she'd been in then. And if she told them her story, reminded them of who she had been, would they thank her? Would they hate her? Or would they merely be reminded of what they'd lost? Did they miss the sun, the moon, the scent of pine trees on the wind? Didn't she? It was difficult to know the true depth of what any of them had traded away. Perhaps by now the war had ended and the homes that were once threatened could swing open to peaceful visitors once again. Who could tell?

The matron's face returned to her, along with the sound

of its voice. She felt again the odd pull that had come over her during their session. December didn't trust it now and didn't trust it then. The outage still bothered her. Malor's story, too, seemed full of holes. If it was difficult for her, with her slightly elevated vantage, to know the truth of her circumstance, to understand the quality of this refuge, how would the purveyor of fine china know the truth of what had been and what was coming? Didn't she have some responsibility to them then?

She couldn't undo her participation in what now felt more like capture. Now that they were here, shouldn't she at least try and disseminate the truth, whatever it may be? December sat at her desk and put together a short letter to her editor, proposing that they meet for lunch.

Back in the kitchen, she made a cup of tea and looked over the assignments once again. A sale on umbrellas was usual enough. In the summertime, they were a most needed accessory; large, heavy, sharp objects, pieces of hot shrapnel, gears and spent artillery, and big chunks of people fell. Arms, legs, the chassis of people falling made walking in the city unprotected dangerous. You could break a neck and spend the next week in the hospital having your parts reprinted. So, throughout the summer season, you needed to carry a good, strong umbrella with you everywhere you went. In the winter, the weather faded. Only ash, bits of paper and cloth floated down. You could get away with just a hat. So as demand for umbrellas fell, so too did the price, and she understood that sellers wished to move their inventory to make room for next year's models.

What December didn't recognize were the machetes and the boots. She had never seen them advertised and didn't immediately understand their utility. The city's streets were paved well and she didn't know anyone with a riotous garden. What need did the people of Pluto City have for a massive garden blade? Unless there was a need. Unless the ads themselves were the story the lumens wished to tell.

The apprehension chilled her. Maybe the paper was already responding to the current events. What if the story she imagined needed telling was occurring not through a direct dispensation of valuable facts and context, but through the products on offer? What if all the people would get in the way of a solid answer was another thing to work for and to buy?

December heard the inbox in her office *ding* and found a fresh sheet of paper spooling into the tray. Her editor had returned her message. She was available to meet.

＝

GILDA'S WAS in the Second District and occupied the windowless ground floor of a twenty-story brick building on the corner of Hate and Moral. The door was heavy and the air whooshed as December pulled it open, as though the building itself were exhaling. Inside, the lights were low. A zinc bar stretched along the left side of the dining room. In the middle there were circular tables bearing little candles, and on the right hand side there was a row of crimson-leather booths. It was quiet this time of day and December easily spotted Heather Mercy.

The woman was solidly built. She had one of the expensive bodies. Big-boned and regal. She had installed herself in the booth furthest from the door and sat with her back to the wall, watching December as she approached. She didn't stand to shake December's hand. Instead, she held aloft a cocktail glass as though to toast December and welcomed her to take the seat across.

"Drink?" said Heather.

December had been working for the paper for six winters and had only met with Heather on one occasion, when she had first been hired. She realized in a moment how siloed they all were. How many writers were there even? She didn't know.

"No, thank you," said December as she settled into the plush faux-leather and spread her palms on the table.

"You'd let me drink alone, would you? What a beast," Heather winked. She finished her drink and gestured toward the bar for another drop.

"I appreciate you meeting me on such short notice," said December.

"Of course. I love a lunch. These days, I can't think of a better way to spend one's time."

December realized how unaccustomed she was to banter. She had her reasoning for being here, and so she got right to the point.

"Well, that's actually why I wanted to meet with you. I wanted to talk to you about the latest batch of assignments. About the paper overall these days."

"Oh god, not work. Don't tell me you invited me here to talk about work," she sipped and smacked at the fresh beverage as soon as it arrived. "And here I was thinking this was a social call. That perhaps you wanted to be friends."

Friends. What a word. The concept of a social call seemed far outside her protocol. What was there to do in Pluto City but work? It was as though relations in Pluto City had been frozen, the people held apart in a glacial flow. Such that December couldn't tell if she saw her own loneliness echoed in Heather's bearing or if there was a bit of sarcasm in her voice.

Heather spoke into the silence. "Maybe you'd like some wine? Something not so strong? Yes, that's what you'd like isn't it. Just a little something to take the edge off. I can have them water it down."

No, it wasn't sarcasm December heard. There was a listlessness in Heather's affect. December thought perhaps the memories were returning for Heather, too. What life had she led in the Sun Country? What had she left behind?

"Thank you," said December. "No. I'd really like to talk about the paper. I think it's important, in light of recent events, to understand what it is we're—what it is *I'm* doing."

"You think you should be doing more?"

"Well, yes."

"My goodness, don't be so boring. Work is work. Just do your part and live your life," said Heather.

"But how can I live my life when I'm unsure if the place that contains it will stick around? You know the big story better than I do. This refuge is supposed to be permanent. If that's no longer true, well, I think we have a part to play in letting people know."

"I guess we *are* having this conversation then," Heather said, with a genuine disappointment in her voice. She gestured once more to the bar for another refill and for the first time, it seemed, really looked at December. Her gaze was focused, hungry, domineering. "Tell me, what value do you think that will bring?"

"Well, the outages are happening aren't they? City wide there have been failures. If it's just a temporary dip, that's one thing. But if it's a bigger issue, some problem with the city overall, people should know that. They should have all the information available and then make a choice about what to do with their lives."

"*Their* lives," Heather snorted. Received her beverage and sipped it once more. "First of all it's *fluctuations*. Not failures. If you're going to make me talk about work on my lunch, then I must insist on an accurate treatment. Second, what do you think there is to do?"

"If the power's going out, people should know that so they can get their things in order and leave if they think it's appropriate. That's another promise of the city, isn't it? A refuge from a violent war, yes, but one you can leave at any time. I know the literature."

"Why would anybody want to leave? There's nothing left up there to go to. This is the only game in town."

"How do you know? When was the last time you saw the Sun Country? What if there's something left? For all we know, the war's over," said December.

"I'm wholly uninterested in the conditions of the Sun Country, and I'll tell you why. The only way that war ends is with mutual destruction. Either it's already there or quickly on its way."

"So then there's a chance it isn't gone, that it isn't a wasteland. Hasn't that been the story we all tell, that it's already gone?"

"I won't quibble with you over wrinkles."

"Even so, let's say it's a rotten horror show. The very worst. Don't you think they—that *we*—should be able to make that choice? And don't you think that choice should be an informed one? Informed beyond, I don't know, a new line of products? I just think we deserve more than new things to buy. Flashlights and machetes tell a story, don't they? But it's limited. It limits us, robs us of a more essential choice."

"I don't go in for existentialism. As soon as you start asking questions that don't have answers, you start dreaming things up to satisfy your curiosity, and those things become your worldview. Disagreement abounds. Fights start, then wars, then we're right back where we started. You want to leave? Be my guest, just let me know so I can get someone interested in the job to cover your assignments," said Heather.

"But what if we did real journalism? What if we found the people who have the answers we're looking for and asked them, and published the results? *Some*body has to know what the problem is. Maybe they don't have solutions yet, but I don't think wondering after the ramifications of the present moment is faulty logic. It's real work. The sort of work I'd like to do. I'll maintain my usual assignments, but work at this in my spare time. I'm not expecting any preferential treatment or change to our basic agreement."

Heather sat back. She had become uninterested in her drink. She looked at December. Her eyes narrowed.

"You know, I think I'm beginning to understand what this is all about. You're unsatisfied with your job. You think you're better than it and you see an angle to exploit. Which I can appreciate in a certain sense. I respect the ambition. You won't get very far without it, or wouldn't have in the Sun Country. But this isn't the Sun Country. This is Pluto City, and Pluto City is no place for ambition unless you are prepared to give up more than you'll ever gain. In order to survive here, to survive in any new place, you have to cut off what's inessential and throw it to the dogs."

"I thought you didn't go in for existentialism," December said.

"You've got it good. I hope you realize that."

"Tell me," said December. "Who were you before you

came here? What memories are coming back for you? Because for me—."

Heather held up her hand.

"We aren't friends. You've made that clear. You've arranged this meeting because you wanted something and you've not gotten it, so you want something else instead. Be careful with your wants. Don't confuse them. You want to go off and make people uncomfortable—because that's all you do with this little article idea of yours, reminding people what they don't have—it won't be under the *Sun's* employ. Our job is to remind them what they *do* have. If that's boots and garden tools, so be it. That's your role. That's your job."

"I just think we can do better."

"On what grounds? Who are you to evaluate our work's significance?"

December didn't have a good answer. Not yet. She was surprised by the question. Her face, the quality of her silence, must have betrayed her.

"You are an agent of your employer. You receive the assignments I deem appropriate and you complete them. The consideration of their larger meaning does not fit within the dictates of your function. It doesn't even fit within mine. However what does fall to me is the evaluation of your performance, which is all that keeps you in your little apartment and the dispensation of joules flowing into your account. If you determine this arrangement is insufficient, well you can let me know. Do you understand?"

"Sure," said December. "I think you've made yourself clear."

"Good. I look forward to receiving your articles. Tomorrow morning, before the victory bell. I'll consider any tardiness as notice of your resignation."

"I thought the deadline was tomorrow night."

"Evidently you have more than enough time on your hands," said Heather. "That will be all."

December felt an incandescent rage. She stood without another word and left.

She walked to steady herself, to think. How could the woman sit there and pretend like nothing happened? Or worse. That it had and didn't matter.

SHE REACHED the carousel without incident. The great, squat bulletin board, positioned like a statue at the center of the roundabout where Third, Beacon, and Trench Street intersected. This was in the Third District, her home district. It had panes of glass for digital advertisements and variegated swatches of faux-cork where people could post their personal ads for services rendered, coupons, salutations, and reflections. The panels, each rotating after a slow interval, to offer more real estate. A crowd, as always, was gathered. Reading. Pulling sections of paper off to take home with them and later redeem. She observed a young girl approach the carousel, with her scuffed shoes and soft cheeks, looking upward as if praying to an advertisement for silk gloves.

This was where, in the early days, December had posted her writing. Back then, she had been attending small arts performances on her own, publishing her little writings to the boards around town, tacking them up for anybody who was interested to read. Pluto City was not flooded with such provisions in those years. In those years, people were hungry for any writing that reflected them, that suggested what it meant to live in their new world.

December breathed. The city was concealing something, the quality of its refuge shifting. She could feel it just as strongly as the impression she had of feeling responsible for those she had convinced to come here. The catalog that employed her wanted nothing to do with printing anything of real value. Fine. That didn't mean she couldn't write it and post it herself. Yes, she thought, this was how she'd play it. She'd carry out the assignments she was given, and then she'd write her own collection and post it anonymously where anybody walking by could read.

What Heather didn't know about was her connection to Malor. However little she felt like seeing him, she had to admit how much more interesting what he'd told her before his race now seemed. Buoyed by the thought, she made her way back to her apartment.

When December returned, she completed the assignments as Heather Mercy had given them to her—she felt, dimly, that her safety depended on it—and slipped into her bed. She didn't so much sleep as shut down; rest did not rise up and caress her. Rather she had the experience of wakefulness followed by an end to her senses. And when she woke, she was greeted by Pluto City once again, a moment later. The day song. Sound of honking traffic and busy people moving about their tasks and functions.

# SIX

DECEMBER COUNTED five nights since the ritual of Malor's faux-sacrifice and figured that by now he had completed his recovery. She made her way to his apartment. While he could have lived anywhere in the city he liked, in a high-rise in the Second District or even in one of the mansions in the First, he chose to live in the Third. He felt it made him seem more grounded, though he still owned the entire building that he called his home.

As she made her way down Beacon, she saw two matrons, walking side by side. They were walking toward one of those vagabond types who slept without a house, who called the streets of the city their own. As the matrons reached him, she was reminded of the city's goodness—that at least there were those that one could talk to when they were feeling untethered.

But when the matrons reached him, they did not bend to talk to him kindly as she had seen them do before. They put their hands on him. She heard the man yell. They covered his mouth. They pulled him, unwilling, to his feet. He let his body go limp and collapsed to the ground in protest. The matrons sort of shrugged, then one of them opened the red robe and the other lifted the man by his midsection. He tried to kick but its arms were too strong. The matron forced him into the open robe, as though it were an open mouth, and the man was gone. He had been swallowed.

She kept walking, gripped by a sudden panic.

On the corner of Beacon and 3$^{rd}$ was the brick building that housed, on the ground floor, a drinking tavern, an antique store showing in its window, hung by strings, hand-carved masks. A small hand-painted sign advertising that all of the items sold here were Made in Pluto City. Both closed to business at this hour, but next to this, the illuminated sign of a fortune-teller. The window had been recently broken, little glass diamonds spread upon the sidewalk. December paid it little mind, her thoughts captured now by what she had seen happen to the rough sleeper. She scanned the upper floors, a cracked hallway window, from which came a milky yellow glow, two cigarette-burned mannequins with decorated faces, nailed to the wall. Yes, this was the one.

Inside, soft music threaded the hallway, the ceiling tall. Malor's assistant Gist was playing night manager. He wore a chiseled body and an open robe, eyes fashioned to be sharp, though dulled by certain habits of his insides.

"December V. Good to see you again so soon."

"Is he here?"

Gist shook his head.

"Tommy's?"

Gist nodded.

The tavern. Where Malor went when he was feeling haunted.

The door pulled open easily. The lights were low. Dark even. On the left side, a long, scratched-up wooden bar. In the middle some circular tables with little red lanterns on them. Along the right side, a row of booths upholstered with a shiny red material.

December noticed, absently, yet for the first time, that the layout was precisely the same as Gilda's. The shape, the contour of it like an echo; the only difference was the material hung upon the chairs, the tables, the material of the bar itself. And the patrons. Rather than the coiffed and well-dressed executives you'd find having a meal and a cocktail in the Second District, the people gathered here wore dark, thin fabric, and didn't speak to one another, as though each were drowning in a pool of his own making.

One of them, sat hunched over a glass of imitation lager, was Malor. The seat next to him was open and December took it. He didn't look over to her until she spoke.

"Ember, you came," he said as though he had invited her.

"I just saw the matrons, they dragged a man off the street," she said.

The surprise and pleasure in Malor's eyes quickly extinguished. He returned his attention to his drink.

"They've been revised," he said, looking into his glass. "Apparently they were involved in some colossal data breach."

December thought of her meeting with the matron, not so long ago now, when it had prompted her to look into her past for the source of her guilt. She thought it prudent not to mention; Malor's connection to the city's founding family had always made her wary. However much of an outcast he had become, shirking, she was sure, some essential role for him his father, Remy Pendegast, would have wanted, blood was blood. Or circuitry was circuitry.

"How've you been," she asked. "Last I saw you, you were in pieces."

"They put me back together, same as always. Though every time I feel a little less," he finished his beer. Ordered another. The barkeep asked for her order and she shook her head.

"Well it's good to see you," she said. "It's good to see a familiar face."

"Is it?" he asked. "Am I really so familiar?"

"As much as I hate to admit it, you're the only friend I have," she said.

"Well isn't that depressing," he said, without the question mark.

"More and more I feel I know so little about who I am or what this place is, but I figured I would try."

"That's the spirit. How's the catalog?" he asked, ribbing her.

"You know, I think that's what it really is. I think you were right," she said.

"It's a joke, December. I think what you do is grand."

"I don't know," she said. "I think I felt like my contribution was worth something, that I was a part of making a fuzzy life more clear, but now. Yeah. I just wrote three advertisements for little objects and the power's going out in the city and nobody knows why and we're all just walking around like it isn't happening."

"Well, it doesn't really matter anyway, does it?"

"I've been hearing that a lot lately. It's actually why I came to see you. The other night I didn't have the ears to listen to you, but I'm curious now."

This seemed to cause him pain. He sipped his beer and grimaced.

"You were right not to. I don't know what I was thinking."

"Look," she said. "I don't think the paper's going to bite on any pitch regarding the outages, but that doesn't mean we have to be silent."

Malor's shoulders dipped. He mumbled.

"What was that?"

"I said the silence will become us."

"I'm serious. I want to help."

"Oh yeah?" Malor said with a wry grin. "What changed for you?"

"The lights going out have caused some memories to return and now I feel somewhat responsible."

"For what?"

"For this," she gestured to the bar, the rows of gleaming bottles, meaning the maybe-city maybe-prison going dark.

"Well just be patient. When the lights go out, so will we. Then it'll be over. Won't be long."

He had said it so casually that at first December took it in stride, but then the meaning caught.

"What'd you say?"

"When the lights go out, we will too. All this searching, all this death we've been avoiding coming here will finally find us, make us honest, make us whole."

"Do you know this or is this just you being glum?"

"I don't know, you know my family. Sometimes I hear things."

"Then why aren't they telling anybody? Why are they pretending like nothing's happened?"

Malor shrugged, once again losing his energy to perform.

"And if that's something the lumens really know, like if

that's true, then we should be putting that out there so people can get their affairs in order."

"What's the point in that?"

"Malor what's wrong with you? How can you be so cold? Wasn't it you, just the other night, talking all high and mighty about taking up your father's mantle? Where'd that guy go?"

"I died. You saw me. You saw me in pieces on the road," he said.

"But you didn't. You're here."

"Exactly!" he said. "It didn't matter. Didn't matter then and doesn't matter now. You'd be better off just accepting it. The experiment failed and we're stuck and we're not getting out."

"If there's still power, power enough to light the place, there's still time to get to the station. Have you been back to the Sun Country yourself? Do you know it's really all gone?"

"I'm a sacrificial lamb. That's all any of us ever are."

"I'm beginning to remember why we broke up," she said.

"Let's not go there."

"No really, you sit here with all your power and all your access, sinking into your glass. It's like anybody who knows anything is just sitting here, like this, like you are, drinking away the day."

Malor didn't speak.

"Why don't you ask them, I mean really ask them. Your father and whoever else."

"I haven't seen my father in years," said Malor.

"Well let me meet them. Set up a meeting with them and let me ask. We have a right to know."

"Nobody's going to talk to you. Not anybody with any

idea of what's really causing this. I don't even know if they do."

"If the problem's in the Sun Country then they can fix it. All I'm seeing is a failure of the will," said December.

"Maybe they just want to let it die. Maybe they don't care about you, or me, or anybody, December. Maybe it's best you just accept that, go along living your little life until it's over. I should be doing more. I know that," said Malor. "But at the same time, I know there isn't anything to do."

She saw in Malor yet another wall, as he had always been to her when it mattered. The brand of acceptance he was expressing struck her as offensive now. Collaborators in malaise, he and Heather.

"You haven't even got a face," December said. "No wonder I can't see you."

And with that, she left. The streets were empty of people this time of night. She marveled, darkly, at how quickly he could pull her into his mood. How it felt as though she had been pulled to the bottom of a sea within her. She knew it had been a mistake to visit him, that of course he'd have nothing for her. When she walked the streets now, she noticed only the doors. Closed to her, locked tight, and the outages taking on an existential quality —that when the circuitry of the city went cold, so would she.

# SEVEN

TWO NIGHTS HAD PASSED since December met with Malor, two nights since she had seen the matrons eat a man, and in that time she had not ventured out of her apartment. She could see, from her kitchen window, that whole buildings were now without power. Their outlines stood as darkened absences, where not a brick remained. How long until her own shelter disappeared into the nothing?

The evernight, that which held the city, was understood as unmitigated cyberspace, a blank thing, onto which the foreboding character of the unknown was projected. Now that the lights had cracked enough times, it was as though this mystery, this antimatter, was leaking into the streets and into its people, into her, into her conception of herself. Carrying along with it memories, yes, but what to do with them, what it meant to now grapple with them was what she couldn't understand.

She felt as though she was a half-person, composed of half-truths. Of unfinished sentences, or broken lines of code. The story went that this city was a simulation, that everything around her, this body, too, was stored on servers.

Sun Country wasn't distant, then. She was still in it, contained in what she imagined was a black box in some rack in some temperature-controlled room. Ultimately flattened, rendered into electrical impulses traveling along tiny lengths of copper—or was it gold? She didn't know the true materiality of her existence.

Maybe the problem with the power existed at the very source. Maybe after all the war was ending, not in peace but in annihilation, just as the big story suggested, coming true like prophecy, and whatever powered the servers that held them, that held the city, was sputtering now, breathing its last, out of reach, untouchable, impossible to resuscitate.

December moved through the rooms of her apartment. She sat on her couch and gazed at the painting on the wall before her, composed of mostly deep reds and pinks, an abstracted scene, more the memory of a feeling than a story. The foreground like the face of a steep hill, decorated with sprays of dark green, and atop the vast red pink purple ridge, the outline of individual warriors assembled in a line, made up of the same pink and red of the ridge, brilliant against a deep blue twilight, the points of their rifles and the horse of the leader starkly outlined. The warriors were poised as though on the precipice of a battle, as though they watched an advancing army, or as though they were the first wave of the advancing army, but frozen in decision, subdued by a feminine repose.

When she stood closer to the piece, when she inspected the piece more closely, she could see the small droplets of black paint on the varied pink and red and blue and how the artist had allowed the color to drip together, as though it had been spilled onto the canvas and allowed to run together, and allowed to dry and then been scratched at with a tiny, sharp-tipped instrument. The assembled figures, above her head—she looked up to see them, as though she was herself a part of the scene—had taken into them the color of the land but through a kind of emulsion, some chemical reaction that formed the color into circles, with coronas of white, a blooming, bubbling characteristic. The flat brim of the leader's hat sharp against the deep blue, fading twilight, giving over to a lighter turquoise around the ankles and the rifle butts, their barrels extending at an angle above the shoulders, held at the ready, fit to aim, but patient. A beauty before the violence, or perhaps before the turning away. The painting allowed for this potential, as though the figures might turn and leave the fight behind them and choose instead to fade into the blue. If only she could see their faces. Then she would know their intent and guess at what her future held.

Was the painting a reproduction? An artifact of the Sun Country copied and pasted onto her apartment wall? Perhaps every apartment wall in the city held one, each room the echo of another, just as each of us were. A copy of a copy of a copy, ad infinitum, like glimpsing yourself in between two mirrors, arm lifting to wave to the marionette at the end of the hall, the gesture returned automatically, not out of feeling, but of a distant command, obeyed automatically by not a person but a figment. Or had the painting been made here, the pigment itself borrowed, a replicant of something real, yet organized here by a local hand, shaped and given life?

The big story said that this city was all there was, that for this inheritance they were lucky. The big story scorned the dead and scorned those who had allowed themselves to be caught out in the cold, who didn't reach the cave's mouth before the boulder was rolled into place to seal the entrance, as the storm prevailed. The big story was insufficient, its warmth and light too weak to see one another's faces, the particularity of expression, the texture of hope and pain.

The big story said that they could leave, but why hadn't she?

And when she asked herself this question, she couldn't hear the answer. It was as though a part of her was speaking from the bottom of an ocean. She could tell that it was there, buried in the depths of her, intelligible only by the bubbles popping on the surface.

Why stay? She asked, simply. This time, there were no bubbles. No calling out, no reaching. In this silence, she had her answer. She looked around her apartment then with a fresh perspective. Was there anything that she would miss? Counting up the objects, they felt as numbers do, slender things, shaped by logic, for which she felt no love. Well, then which of her possessions held utility? Her passport. Yes, her passport.

As such, the plan was born. Made of little questions and the evidence of little answers, the shape of which she held lightly in her palms, obvious to her now. The anger she had felt for Heather had worn off. The credulity she lent Malor light as breath. If the paper wouldn't print it, if no one with any knowledge of the outages would speak to her, then she would have to get outside the place to find a semblance of the truth.

She headed for the station.

December was on Manger when the block went out. This time, as the last, the seconds, minutes, hours, however long it lasted, was uncountable, but felt longer. More complete. She stood and shut her eyes, as if it would make a difference to her visibility, feeling the hard concrete beneath her feet give way to a softer material. When she opened her eyes again, there was the blankness. A total lack of light. However the longer she stood, her eyes adjusted. She looked down at her feet and could just make out the outline of the tip of her shoe. She stepped forth, scuffing her heels against the soft material beneath her, and when she did, she kicked up a puff of green, bioluminescent dust, which settled quickly and dropped once more into gray darkness. She was bending to her knees to touch the material when the lights, and with it the city, flickered back. The street, the buildings that lifted into the evernight sky, with them the sound of the city and the night song returned, and with it the memory.

━━━

ON HER LAST night in Mirror Bay, the night of her transfer, the storm had returned, bringing with it thunder and lightning. When the power went out, August and December lit candles and sat together in the living room. She could remember a tense quietness in her father's bearing, as though he was angry with her. Maybe he had been scared. Maybe he had known what was coming and had not told her. A week prior, a big gray ship had appeared on the horizon. A Theo vessel, it was said. The metal gunship floated there, belching its cloud of diesel into the sky, and without anybody from the ship coming onshore, there was no news to speak of. August and December had carried on their work, as usual, until this night, when the alarm rose, a sharp wail, piercing through the rain

Before she could understand what was happening, they were running through the night, toward the natatorium. And it was there that she and August parted ways. He had lifted her into the big chair in the deep end of the pool, and though the power was out here, too, the machine had its generator full and with that power he had got the paddles going and hurriedly input the coordinates.

He hadn't the time to numb her, so she felt every bit of the cool steel rods, boring into the length of her spine. The night was blurry now, but the memory of waking in the train, a sort of dream, in which she was not herself but someone else remained.

It was day. A platter of the morning sun slid across the table at her booth. Out the window, amber waves of grain flicked by.

She had the sense, immediately, that the train was very long, and that she sat near the front; if she were to stand and walk forward, in the direction the train was moving, it would take her only one partition to reach the conductor, and he would be sitting on a red wooden chair, and his face she would not know. She knew that in the cars behind her were kept all her memories, held in instances of fine luggage, in leather-bound trunks and embroidered valises, in armoires and armored boxes. Better yet the articles therein, the silk, chiffon, lamé, corded gold trousers and rare-earth tiaras spoke to her of aristocracy. In fact, this train was hers, a bracelet run round her wrist.

She was not alone. Down the lilting car sat a young boy, maybe thirteen, maybe her age, the age she thought she'd been. He wore a dusty brown suit and had dirty knuckles and he was smoking. He was smoking a short brown cheroot, and he was taking great pleasure in his smoking, with lazy eyes and a wry smile spread across his lips. He caught her gaze and she knew two things, with a creamy certainty, as one does in dreams: she was in fact a duchess, run away from home; the requirement foisted upon her by an overbearing father and blithely expectant mother, to marry and carry on the name were unfit for her constitution and the loss of her sister didn't make it any better; the second thing she understood was people come and go. She carried this bit in her, wrapped in gauze, able to feel the sharp contours by reputation more than bite. It made the center of her heavy, down where the quiet voice bloomed.

The air shrieked and howled as behind her an attendant entered, sliding open the door between two cars. He barreled toward the boy who had been smoking, who had since stanched his cigar. December, who was not December, stood and imposed upon the thin white suit.

"Leave him be. He's with me," and her voice was older, it was oily and subsistent and as the woman who was not December spoke, the sunlight flickered down and the train car filled with ample dark. All was silent, as for a moment the car floated—it had run off the edge of the world and now hung for a moment above the volume. And then it plunged, down through star, down through night, sending December's stomach up. And through the evernight the train had run, reaching its terminus in Pluto City, where her new life began. She had awoken in the hospital, hooked up to a transfer machine, the memory of the train dissipating.

Now, walking to the train station once more, to ride it back into the life she had left behind, back to the Sun Country, she felt as though she were completing a kind of circuit. She wondered, too, if it would still be dangerous. Perhaps the town of Mirror Bay had been reoccupied, and she would find herself immediately apprehended, hurt, tortured. She allowed herself to feel the fear for just a moment before allowing a certain pleasure to come from its presence. If it were in fact dangerous, it would be proof that she was no coward for leaving the city now. Whatever she found out, if she survived, she'd bring back.

The station occupied a large courtyard, paved with

large adobe tiles. December heard the crowd before she rounded the corner. The people, all Third District-types, shop owners and waitresses, mechanics and drivers, gathered in loose lines, waiting to reach one of the attendants who stood behind the glass partitions of the ticket office. Behind the ticket office was the platform. Steam rose from beyond the low wall. December could not see the train, but she knew it was there, and felt as though she had arrived, just in time.

But the lines weren't moving. From the outskirts of the crowd, she could hear the ripples of discontent. Voices rising and falling jaggedly.

"What's going on?" December asked the woman standing nearest her, who wore the compact body of an electrician and a panic she recognized in her face. December wondered, suddenly, if she had known her in Mirror Bay, if she had been one of her clients.

"They aren't letting anybody leave," said the woman. "We haven't had any power at our houses for the last week. They are saying it's nothing to be concerned about, but then why won't they turn back on our lights? Why won't they let us leave?"

December didn't have any answers for the woman, but she had her passport, an object in which she still believed. She pushed her way toward the front of the line.

There were four attendants, identical automations, one at each of the glass partitions, standing impassively. December presented her credentials and the attendant nearest her spoke into the small intercom.

"We have no tickets remaining at this time," said the attendant.

"Well, when's the next train leaving?" December asked.

The attendant asked to see her passport and December fed it through the slot at the bottom of the partition.

"I need the earliest departure you have on the books. It's important," said December, hopefully, as the attendant opened the tiny booklet and scanned it with their eyes.

"You lack the proper clearance," said the automation, and slid December's passport back.

"What do you mean?"

"The earliest departure for your status will likely be next winter," said the attendant, and clicked off the intercom and returned to her impassive stance.

"Why? What's the issue?"

December slapped her hand against the glass, using the heel of her faux palm to rattle it in its frame.

"You have to tell us why," said December. "What's happening?"

The attendant gave up nothing.

December turned back to the crowd, to the hundred or so faces that seemed to look at her expectantly. Again, she wondered, did any of them know her? What did she possibly have to give?

The train whistle sounded and the steam increased, pumping over the low wall of the ticket office. December moved, keeping her head down, walking slowly until she reached the turnstiles that separated the courtyard from the platform. Swiftly, she climbed over them.

Ahead of her, the train. The engine of black metal and twisted pipes. She reached the open door of one of the passenger cars.

Inside, the car was blank. No rows of seats, no carpet, no windows. It was just blank. A white box. A different kind of absence than she was used to. The ground beneath her feet disappeared. And as she kept stepping, she found herself again on the other side of the platform. A dreary cement wall, the chipped stone that lay between the tracks, sharp against the soles of her thin boots.

All she knew to do was keep moving, keep running, down the tracks, away from the train, away from the station. Once she had put the station behind her and carried on, through the residential homes and neighborhoods that were built on either side of the track, she was alone with the buildings and with the chipped stone that made her stumble every few steps.

If the train wouldn't take her to the Sun Country, she would walk it then. She would follow these rails as far as they would take her, to the end of the city and beyond. She consoled herself with a quickly built resilience: this was the beauty of rail travel, that even without the steaming vehicle, one could follow its route to the very end. It might take her longer, but she would arrive at her destination, and she would gather what information she needed, and return to the city with the truth.

The further she walked, the quieter the city became. She entered the newest section of the city, on the very outskirts. A thin, orange, sodium-lit glare made shadows of the stones beneath her feet. She walked in a growing silence until finally she came to the great wall.

And, here, the rails stopped. There was no passage. Just a wall of stone, the terminus of our construction. She felt herself an island. Maybe after all, she was synthetic, too. All of her. Of course she was. Where the city ended, so did she. She felt a hollowness where her soul should be, and with this listless feeling, this ache in her, she faced this island of dying light, and walked back toward the only home she knew.

# EIGHT

THE CITY WELCOMED her with open arms. The ash fell lightly. Just little bits of paper and cloth adorned with very little drops of blood. People walked with their heads down, pacing consistently. Going to work, going to eat, running errands maybe, maybe on the way home to make love. She attempted to make eye contact, to smile, to reach some mutual acknowledgement of their placement here as citizens, as members of the still-living. But it was as though she was invisible, as though she was a ghost.

She ducked into the small shop on Meander where she bought her papers, and saw the usual face. An impassive, large man, with little hands and a quiet disposition. There, next to the sticks of gum and bags of candy, the latest edition of the *Pluto City Sun*. She plucked it from the stand and saw that her advertisements had already been published. She moved to the counter and set the paper down, as she usually did, this movement for her automatic.

"Hi there," she said. "How are you doing today?"

"Two joules," he said. This was their usual conversation. Nothing more, nothing less.

But this day was different. It had to be.

"The ash is lighter today. Lighter than usual, don't you think?" she said.

"Can I get you something else?" said the attendant, merely locating the shape that stood before the counter in his store.

"No, not really. Hey, you know I'm in here every day and I don't even know your name."

"Two joules then for the paper," was all he said, and he returned his eyes to the register, where each day he would type in the number of joules exchanged for the paper. He looked at it, as though all he wanted to do was type in the amount that she had paid, but since December hadn't handed him anything, he couldn't. He was stuck, and in his face, it looked like he was in pain.

"Have you been remembering, too? Where'd you live when you were in the Sun Country? I came from Mirror Bay. My name's December."

December felt a sort of desperation bubbling in her. Somehow she felt more alone here than she had at the limits of the city.

"That'll be two joules," he said, and he smiled. And the smile was terrible.

December left the paper, or the catalog, whatever you called it, on the counter and stepped back into the night. The people outside moved as they always had, each directed by some impulse, or perhaps only by the dictates of their function.

———

ALTHOUGH SHE HAD LEFT the apartment recently, had only been gone from it for the time it took her to reach the station and walk the tracks, December felt as though she was returning from a lengthy journey. She observed her material possessions once more and saw in them only the space between the particles. As though she could reach through them and touch only the absence underneath.

So it was ending. December didn't know when, but it was ending and there was no way out. Not for her, not for the others who had tried to act upon the offer inlaid into the big story that each of them had been told. This refuge was supposed to be forever, as long as we would need it; we were supposed to be able to leave, whenever we would like.

As far back as she could remember, she had been telling that tale. She was subsumed by it. Even in Mirror Bay, this role had become her, and all she'd done since was find another way to do the same. It was as though she were still somehow that little girl, replicating falsehoods, weaving together crooked threads, building cornerstones of nothing to stand upon.

And yet, if everything was truly ending, if the city and everything that mattered was going out, why revise the matrons, why instill a partition between the knowing and the unknowing? There was something the lumens considered worth protecting, worth holding out of sight. Maybe the big Truths were out of reach for her; maybe Malor was right and no one with any influence would speak to her. But what about the small ones?

The big story was made of little stories, each of them like candles, adding up to the larger flame. Maybe it was this that would warm them, maybe it was one another that we were missing, and that by knowing each other, seeing ourselves reflected, not marionettes but people, we could light ourselves toward another door, another exit, once the big story collapsed under the weight of our questions, or of the answers that we held.

December felt the contours of a possibility, reaching out of the dark, and though she couldn't hold it yet, she believed that it was there. Yes, she still wished to know them—be they answers or be they people—to hold her own candle against the dark. Maybe it was the collection and dissemination of their stories that would make her. She would soldier on, as did the city. She could hear it now, going through its motions, the motion itself still possible. For them, for every person in the city, and for her.

As if on cue, her inbox *dinged*. She rushed into her office as though to receive a murmuration from God. She caught the paper as it was spooling out of the slot in the wall.

*"December,"* it began. *"Thank you for executing the last round of articles, and on time no less. I saw no trace of the confusion you expressed to me at lunch.*

*As much as it pains me to say this, your instincts were correct. The paper would like more features, more journalism as you called it. I'd like to see how you handle an assignment with a little more meat on the bone.*

*There was recently an altercation at the transfer station in which some problematic individuals staged a riot. These problem people sabotaged the station. An eyewitness reported to me that this mob broke the windows and destroyed the train and, until it can be repaired, the machine will not be operational.*

*We need to write this in a way that makes clear that these individuals are the reason that departure from Pluto City, at present, will not be possible. Additionally, we need to make clear that this is not the time to leave our fellow citizens behind. Please include the following: 'You have no doubt experienced the fluctuations in the power recently and please understand that every effort is being made to understand who is responsible and deal with them accordingly; if you have any information regarding this, please report it to a matron. It's time for us to band together and protect our home from any and all acts of terrorism.'*

*December, please be aware that this is a significant article and I need this by end of day. There are quotes from the eyewitness attached on the following page. As you can see, I've done most of the reporting here. I really just need you to massage this into a cogent and organized bulletin-style feature. We will be printing this under your name. Moving forward, the paper is going to take a more active role in disseminating important information regarding the safety of the city. Since you expressed a desire for this type of work, I thought of you. Depending on how you handle this, there will be more like it coming quickly down the pike. You have an opportunity here to play a significant part in that effort.*

*Please reply as soon as you've received this, so I know not to assign it to someone else. I look forward to hearing from you. We'll be watching."*

December found that she was sitting on the floor. What she had before her did not match what she had witnessed with her own eyes at the station. She had seen no mob, no anger; she hadn't seen anybody breaking windows. What she had seen was a people gathered out of fear. A fear she herself felt. She read over the letter once more and scanned the quotes on the second page. They echoed the sentiment of Heather's assignment, precisely, as though they had been written by the same hand.

The language struck her. 'Problem person' made her shudder. And the story built around the new designation represented a complete revision of what she had witnessed, flattening the experience these people were having into a threat, leaving no room for why they had wanted to leave.

One thing was apparent. Heather must not have known that December herself had been at the station and seen what it was like herself. Why give the assignment to someone with the power to refute it, to someone you didn't trust? She felt as though she was in Heather's good graces. Maintaining this status and the perspective it granted may then prove to be an advantage. But to what end? If she wrote the article as it was outlined, wouldn't she be harming people?

For those who hadn't been there, a vast majority of the *Sun's* readers, reality would shift and bend into an artifice. A gathering of scared individuals became a mob, simply for attempting to cash in on an essential promise she herself had made during the transfers. To write this would be to criminalize a legitimate fear, to turn the desire for another life into rebellion.

What if she didn't? Heather had made herself clear; December's housing was contingent on her employment. She earned it by delivering on the assignments she was given. The streets were no longer a free place; she had seen the city's outliers being rounded up and taken off against their will. To where, she didn't know, but thinking of it scared her. In Pluto City, could a person be repurposed, turned into something else? Could she be erased?

She worried the floor of her apartment, pacing between the kitchen and the living room. She opened the window that looked onto the city below and listened to the city breathe. She recalled her work in Gracehaven and in Mirror Bay. As a child, she had passed along the lie unknowingly. Her young voice had been co-opted without her knowing that there would be no beaches, no sun, no unfettered building of a new future that reached beyond the power structures that had mired us and rendered us inert. If August knew what Pluto City really was, he hadn't let on. He had stayed committed to the cause, however dubious it was, and passed it through her, made of her an unwitting conduit of manipulation.

Now, she had her wits about her. She understood that if she completed the assignment as it was given, she would be purposely swimming out into the deep waters of complicity, without understanding the strength of the currents, or how the choice would ripple outward, who it would touch.

How does one evaluate the shape of a decision? It was difficult to understand the effect the article would have in the particular. For those who were not at the station: legitimate fear, cast as rebellion. A terrorist act, the likes of which would make them wary of their natural compatriots. Perhaps even a sense of patriotism, or whatever you called allegiance to a city, for staying put. In those who had been there, a mistrust of the *Sun*, a defensiveness against the roving eyes of those who had not yielded to their curiosity, their fear, their will to leave. In the streets, the two cohorts would not be able to identify one another. And so, between them would grow a wedge of variable thickness and visibility. This made a general kind of sense. What was harder to guess at was the meaning an individual reader would find for herself when she opened up her paper.

December was angered by her predicament. She felt stuck. She also realized that if she didn't write the article, someone else would. Whether or not she chose to be involved, some version would hit the paper. The city was a story that we told together, sitting round the fire. As the fire waned, the leaders considered their voice the most important. Didn't matter who gave credence to their report.

December breathed. If she wrote the article as it was given, could she neutralize it somehow? Anything that ran counter to the assignment would not make it past editorial review, and would risk marking her as a problem person herself. But what if she could write, alongside it, something else? She recalled the old days, when she first awoke in the confines of the city, when she had written for herself, posting bespoke little fragments on the carousels across the city. Yes, this was still her game. She'd carry out the assignment she was given, revising the collective memory, blurring and reshaping it into yet another artifice. She'd write it under her name. And then she'd write a counter story, post it anonymously where anybody walking by could read.

She sent a wire to Heather, accepting the assignment. Then she got to work.

On her machine, she typed out the revisionist article as it was given. She gave over to performance, describing the people gathered as a mob, making sure to implicate their moral weakness for attempting to leave behind their brethren here just as they had left behind the people of the Sun Country to carry the burden of the war without us. An essential weakness, born out again. Yes, these were problem people, not like the rest of us. She described how they had destroyed the station, and with it the idea of leaving, consuming it for themselves, selfishly, in thoughtless hunger, more than they deserved.

She wrote to herself, admonishing the questioning of the city, the will to leave it, a problematic abdication of duty to her fellow citizens, along with the sabotage of the station's operation. It was her fault the train was hollow. She wrote as one vomits, painfully, the musculature of the stomach and throat heaving, taking over, until the sick was spread across the page. Once she was finished, she read it over once and sent it off.

Then, from the bottom drawer of her desk she pulled out a stack of paper and a pen. She felt the chair beneath her, felt her feet upon the ground, the suggestion of gravity tenuous, the feel of weight a ruse amidst the lines of code.

*"I know a man who shall remain unnamed,"* she began writing, letting the pen scratch along the page. *"He lives here in the city. He wakes each night and walks to his shop and sells items that are small and important. He is in the business of illumination and his memories are returning. In the Sun Country, he had a wife and a child. They lived together in a house and led a life that, before the war, was peaceful. Sometimes he would lay down and rest while the woman he called his wife debated with the spiders who made their webs in the shower. She would try to coax them away from the danger of the falling water, all the while harboring a fear of the alien creatures. The man could hear all this in her voice, listening from where he lay back on the bed they shared. It made him love her. There is a longing in him to return, not to the Sun Country he left behind, but to the peace that existed before it, to the moments of listening to the woman he called his wife debate with the spiders, to the moments before he was tortured by the soldiers, before his wife was killed, before his daughter disappeared. His life, what he considered most important, was destroyed. There was nothing left to live inside of, no more home to call his own. He saw no sense in a world that would rob this woman of her life, so he foreclosed on it and left. Do you think he came here to avoid destruction? To preserve himself and, in that, to abdicate some responsibility he had to those who chose to remain? Or had he made the assessment that there could be nothing new constructed out of the old world and*

*taken a chance on coming here to make for himself something new?"*

December realized as she wrote that it was impossible to understand exactly why Szewski had left the Sun Country and what he had hoped to gain in Pluto City, or if even hope was the correct word to use in describing his motivation.

*"How could you understand the animation of those who chose the transfer? Each person's reasoning was his own, our own. The lover's reasoning belonged to him, and yet from him it has been concealed, replaced, papered over by the rambling of the big story that cares nothing for him, that wishes to impress upon his character its meaning. What else had comprised the man's life? I do not know. To color outside the lines of the sketch I have given you here, all I know of his life before he came to Pluto City, would be an act of speculation. We would have to project something of our own to make up for what is missing. The same goes for probing more deeply beyond, to reach beyond the given page for the reasoning of the reader standing next to you, their hopes and fears, that which led them to this city, and would lead them out of it. We can't know. So be wary of what you read; be wary of the all-encompassing story. Question the motivation for the prevailing narrative when it reaches beyond what can be grasped and felt only by you, within yourself."*

She ended it there. She made two copies of the story, writing each by hand, one for the carousel in the Third District, one for the carousel in the Second. She folded them into the pocket of her coat, then wrapped the coat around her shoulders, the dark fabric lapping at her like the waters of a rising tide, and stepped into the night.

THE DOGS WERE BARKING in the night song. It was near to midnight. December felt the slight weight of the folded papers in the left hand pocket of her coat. She could hear them crinkle a little with each step.

She reached the carousel in the Third District. There were a number of Missing Persons reports, with hand-drawn renderings of the person missing. There were poems written from memory. December found an open swatch of cork and placed one copy of the article there. She did it quickly and walked away, toward the Second District.

The people she walked past held their eyes forward and a little upward, as though their paths had been ordained. Some held umbrellas to keep the slight ash from trickling into their hair. Others wore hats. Even for winter, the ash was light. Barely even a piece as big as the corner of a burnt page fell.

She passed by the hospital, a photocopy of a Sun Country monolith, with all the windows lit, that was appropriately quiet for this time of year, when the injuries from the falling refuse lessened.

December wondered how many of them lived here. The busiest days at the transfer station in Gracehaven saw fifteen or twenty people make the trip. This was before August had taken on the new technic body. This was during a particularly violent six month stretch of the war, when the people who called on them needed very little coaxing. Then, they had used the incinerator for the emptied bodies, wheeling them on gurneys to the furnace door. In Mirror Bay, the work was slower. The busiest day there saw ten souls relieved of their corporeal vulnerability, their future there interrupted and replaced.

Over the three or so years they worked the stations, then, probably two-thousand people crossed Pluto City's threshold. She knew there were other stations, at least one more in Old New York, that city which had defied renaming. Another in Three Notches, in the southern end of what had once been California. And how long had she been here now? How many years had passed since she made her own trip to this peopled void? And in that time, had the program continued? Could it be said that ten-thousand called Pluto City home? Or twenty? Or twenty more?

December tried to picture twenty-thousand people. In order to see them all at once, she needed them to stand still, and she needed to stand above them, looking down. The image before her took on the quality of a gathering army, lined up in organized columns, facing forward, ready to be counted, their willingness implied. Was this any way to see a people?

As December crossed into the Second District, where the engineers and builders and managers lived, where the buildings rose taller and sparkled with inset fixtures, glinting against their glass and steel and polished marble foreheads, she did not hear the soft swishing of the robes behind her and did not realize she was being followed until the matron spoke. The clicking, popping gramophone voice close behind her, yet distant as if it came from the far end of a long, dark hallway.

"Stop walking, you there, in the coat."

And all at once, three matrons encircled her on the sidewalk and made her still.

"May we see your identification?" said another in its matching voice.

December was not carrying her passport, that document one received on arrival, that updated each year with place of residence and employment. All she had was the remaining folded page of her counter story.

"I'm afraid I don't have it on me," she said, forcing her voice to be steady.

"There is no reason to be afraid," said the matron. The three red-robed figures inched toward her, their porcelain, impassive faces showing no expression but the vague, slightly open-mouthed smiles.

"Do you live here in the Second District?"

"My home is in the Third," said December.

"On what business do you call?"

Before December could answer, another of the three spoke.

"State your name and employer."

"December Valence," she said. Her level of compliance shocked her, how smoothly the answers came, as though the matrons were tugging the words out of her. "I write for the *Pluto City Sun.*"

The matrons metabolized the information. She could hear the faint clicking and pushing steam as they reorganized their voices.

"Valence, yes, the image matches. She has good marks. But it says here you were just recently at the carousel. Why was that?" another asked.

"I," December tamped down the flow of words that would reveal her. "I thought I'd do a little reading."

"A little reading. Very well. And what brings you to the Second District?"

"The restaurants are better here," she said. This was true.

Once again the clicks and pops and little puffs of steam rose from inside the three robes.

"Are you still harboring doubt about the nature of the power fluctuations?"

"Of course not," said December, "I trust the leadership, wherever they go we go."

"Noted. Very well."

"Enjoy your feeding."

In the distance, the night song switched its tenor. The midnight tone, the screaming man cried out.

"Move along," said one of the matrons.

December nodded. She made her way up the street. The matrons stood and watched her. She took a right on Foresight and ducked into the first shop she saw, a creamery called David's. She ordered a scoop of the first flavor she saw and sat at a table furthest from the window. She couldn't eat. She lifted one scoop to her lips and then watched the rest of the imitation ice cream melt. She didn't risk the second carousel. She took the folded page from her pocket and dropped it to the floor and left.

# NINE

THE MEMORY OF PORSCHE, released in the latest outage, washed over December like the waters of a flood. She was in the natatorium once more, in Mirror Bay, with her father, with August. The afternoon sun reclined on the horizon, casting a warm and even hue onto the transfer machine as they cleaned it. She was polishing the little screen on the console; he was running a rag over the long, tensile needle where it hung at the back of the chair. This must have been some time after Milo's transfer. She had settled into her role as his assistant and by now she had begun to sense a wrongness in their work, something wordless and intuitive bubbling in the back of her mind. The rusted metal door across the room squeaked and echoed as Porsche pulled it open and there she was. Seven or eight years older than December, lithe and pretty in spite of the deep old scar in the meat of her cheek. She wore the uniform of a Theo raider, the brown camouflage, ill-fitting, bunched in places, torn and resewed in others, stained with aged blood.

Porsche didn't need convincing. She had no ears for

August's pitch, no eyes for the pamphlet, having already concluded that the only thing left for her was the transfer.

"You don't need to do all that," she had said, cutting August off as he was ramping up. "I'm tired of stories. I'm tired of being told what to do and who to hurt, of carrying around the understanding that I'll be hurt if I don't. You can keep the fancy body. I'm done with this place."

"Very well," said August. "But I'm afraid you'll have to wait. It has been a busy day. The battery needs charging."

He indicated the generator in the corner of the room, its diodes showing orange.

"Would you like to come home with us for dinner?" December said.

And so the three of them walked the route through Mirror Bay to the house on Chief Street, fending off the scowls from those who saw them all together. This was a Technocrat town, had been for several years now; to them, Porsche's uniform made her out to be their enemy. December noticed the way they looked at her, from the porches of their homes, the way anyone they passed on the sidewalk crossed the street, avoiding them, repulsed, and the way that Porsche's back remained upright. December admired her self-possession, even then.

As they sat together in the kitchen, lifting spoonfuls of lentil soup, all but August, who didn't eat, Porsche told them a little of her story. She had lost both her parents when she was little. They had disappeared when she was four.

"I can remember feeling really afraid, like there was no one who could protect me. And so as soon as I was old enough to lift a rifle, I did. I got a lot of practice in the early days, keeping eyes on the barbed wire fencing around our compound. There was always somebody trying to climb over, to climb in or climb out. I did it enough that it got to feel normal. I got so used to being war's digestive enzyme that I got around to thinking that's all I was, or all I am."

Porsche had forgotten about her soup. She stared at something December and August couldn't see. Her body wouldn't need the nutrients for long, December thought.

"But then I realized somewhere between Three Notches and Silver Springs that who I was, who I could be, was up to me, that there must be something left inside worth saving. All the years before my birth and all the years after had compressed me into something I wasn't, and if I could just be free of that pressure, what could I do? Maybe open up a restaurant, maybe paint. I don't know. It's something I feel I couldn't do no matter where else in this country I go. No matter where I go here, I'll be flattened by the same old history. So here I am, with you people and your machine, this new city that you hold."

After dinner, August offered her the couch and Porsche accepted. But she didn't sleep. December watched her through the slats in the staircase, keeping quiet, holding her breath. Porsche sat on the couch with her straight back, watching the candles on the mantle burn and drip their wax.


DECEMBER FELT a melancholy sort of gratitude that, out of all the memories, it was Porsche's that returned to her. Two nights had passed since she had submitted her revisionist article, along with her freelance missive, and in that time she had received no new assignment, no communique from Heather. This was unusual. The cadence of her work for the *Sun* was daily. The silence made her nervous. She checked her inbox constantly. She didn't dare leave her apartment, choosing instead to pace her apartment, to steal glances onto the street below, to look for roving packs of matrons. In writing the counter article, and posting it for public eyes, had she marked herself as a problem person and had they found her out? Were they waiting on the street to snatch her?

She realized that the bodily safety she had always felt in Pluto City had dissolved. A core tenet of the city had been violated, such that she wondered if the city was ever really safe, or if in fact it had always been laying in wait for you to put a foot wrong, to step out of line, to make yourself vulnerable to consumption. This was the dynamic that pervaded life in the Sun Country, that which Porsche had lived through and eventually moved past. It wasn't as though she had ever really felt safe, and it was her defiance against it that had inspired December when they met all those years ago.

And yet, the self-possession that Porsche had carved out for herself came at the cost of others' safety. It would be childish to ignore the fact that Porsche had been a killer. Maybe not all the way through into her bones, but the armor she had composed for herself was made of corpses. December had known this even then, even as a child, and now she felt Porsche's complicity in a broken world was, in part, like an echo of her own. She found a sort of strength in this, a connection in the furnace room of moral ambiguity, in the dark where the point was to survive.

The morning after she met Porsche, December had slept long. When she woke the sun was high and bright and the house on Chief Street had been empty. December dressed quickly and rushed to the natatorium and when she arrived, Porsche was already gone. August had finished with the transfer and disposed of her spirit's armor, the body she had commanded in spite of the Sun Country's crushing weight.

Why had December been so sad? Had she wanted to say goodbye, to hold onto this older woman, who could have been a sister or a friend? Perhaps it was Porsche who had planted the seed for December's own desire to emigrate to Pluto City, to start anew, if, after all, the choice had been hers. She didn't fully know. Just as the walls of the city rose upon the limit with the evernight, grand and impenetrable, partitions rose within December that held her separate from whole regions her self.

WHEN THE INBOX in her office *dinged* she rushed to take the paper as it spooled out of the slot in the wall. A momentary relief washed over her when she saw that it was from Heather. However the message was terse and offered no assurance. *December, please meet me at my residence* and her address was all the paper held.

December felt the facsimile of cortisol rush in her imitation bloodstream, the impression of a heartbeat quickening. She measured Heather's language for any hint at her intention and, finding none, assumed the worst, that Heather had discovered her anonymous article, and if the matrons were able to track her movements well enough to place her at the carousel, as they had revealed to her in the Second District, it was only a matter of time until they discovered her little aberration, and so planned to eat her up.

Then again, what if they hadn't? What if Heather's message was merely neutral? If that was true, denying it would bring suspicion.

What would Porsche do?

———

HEATHER MERCY'S apartment was on the sixth floor of the same building that housed Gilda's. December rode the burnished elevator up, watching the brass hand mounted above the door wave over the numbers. Two, three, four, five, *ding*.

The hallway floor was richly carpeted, hushing her footsteps as she made her way to Heather's door, which hung slightly open. Still, she knocked.

"Come in!" the voice was distant, betraying the size of the apartment before December even glimpsed it. She pushed the heavy door open and entered. And it really was a fine apartment. December was impressed. Cork-tile floors and walls of a kind of old-world metal. Jade-colored accent lighting and rich browns and blues. A large mirror in the foyer, reflecting the warm hues. Heather was waiting for her in the living room, sat on a soft-leather couch, where the windows stretched floor to ceiling. She was alone as far as December could tell and this relaxed her. On the center island between the couch and two tasteful chairs sat two cocktails, the glass still frosty.

"Come in and sit," Heather said, indicating the chair across from her. "I appreciate you coming all this way."

December had half-expected to be accosted once again by the matrons when she crossed over into the Second District, as though stepping foot into this more rarefied side of the city would trigger some traitor-alarm system, like the tendrils of an invisible spider web, and send the hungry creatures to spin her up and paralyze her. She had carried this impression with her all the way up the elevator, down the hall, and into this room, feeling as if each step risked the reverberation that would mean her end, practicing along the way her apology, running versions of the conversation over and over again in her head, repeating it like a prayer, all the while knowing it wasn't them that she owed any apology, yet unable to stop hoping she'd be spared.

But Heather's welcoming bearing, that she was welcome in this fine abode, told the version of a story that calmed her. At least enough to sit and accept the cold cocktail, to bring it to her lips and sip, as though she was taking communion, the initiation rites of a new faith.

There was a fresh copy of the *Sun* on the table, her revisionist article above the fold on the front page. She couldn't help but note her byline, her own name, right there in print, and feel good about it. Heather caught her looking and grinned.

"It's a good article, December. I didn't even have to touch it up," she said. "Products are facts, just as facts are products. The equation runs both ways. It's beautiful, the symmetry of our situation, the meaning we give them and the power it grants us to care for them. There is no refuge for anyone without the basic agreement that this city and its facts, its products, are all we have and all we'll ever need."

Pride and guilt mixed in her like oil and water. December felt a thick sort of relief spread into her shoulders, along with a sick tremor in her imitation stomach, some quiet voice in her she drowned out.

"Well I'm glad to be of service," said December, duplicitously happy to be considered inner-circle, spared, not an outlier, part of the elevated whole. "I look forward to helping more."

"That's just the thing I hoped you'd say," said Heather. "Things are getting interesting. There's a new version of the city coming down the pike, and I've been instructed to welcome you along. I was petty to you last time we met, but I'm glad you said your piece. If you hadn't, we would not be sitting here. I hope you take a moment to pat yourself on the back; I didn't realize what sort of asset I had waiting in the wings. You've made me look very good."

December swallowed the rest of her drink and set the sweating glass on the folded newspaper, watched the wet ring spread onto the page. How easy it is to submit when illusion takes on the quality of matter, when you sense the weight of it in your palm.

"Tell me then. What's next?" said December.

"Let me freshen your drink," said Heather.

"Sure, why not."

"That's my girl."

As Heather busied herself momentarily with the clattering and pouring of another round, December found she had no immunity to her charm. She admired the apartment and the comfort of her chair. Very suddenly she had been overtaken, snuggled warmly in the embrace of acceptance and esteem.

"Unification," Heather began. "Unification is the word on which we build our new city. And to that end, we'll need to remind the people, not only of the war they left behind, but of why the war was necessary. The virtue of the fight will be our brand."

Over the course of two more cocktails, Heather laid out the plan, telling December what she needed to know and nothing more. A new boxing league was to be established, featuring a series of matches between the heroes and their antagonists.

"We need to build up a people's champ, somebody all of them can get behind. Her name will be Mona. Mona Kabang. The first fight is in a week's time. Are you interested in conducting an interview and reporting on the fight?"

"Definitely," said December. "Of course."

"Very good," said Heather. "Very good indeed."

At some point, December stumbled back to her apartment, drunk on time and free of spirit.

# TEN

THE NIGHT of Mona Kabang's fight arrived. December felt as though she had become two half-people. A willful propagandist, swaddled in acceptance and approval and the safety it conferred; a deeply scarred little girl rocking back and forth in the corner of a closet with a candle in her hand. There had been no room for this latter half when she had sat with Heather, conspiring over drinks. A comfort then that now had gone, the rift within her exposed as the balmy liquid receded.

She made her way toward the outskirts of the Third District, toward a makeshift venue near the great wall, a bar called the Blurry Mice. On her way to the venue, she stopped at the carousel. She wanted to see if her freelance article was still posted, to perhaps measure its effect in the faces of a reader.

A reassurance she had taken from her meeting with Heather was that she had not been discovered. She had been steeped in this relief. However now it seemed as though the article had never happened. What effect had she hoped that it would have? A riot in the streets? No, not quite. December had not attached any specific expectation to her work, but she did hope that it would ripple outward and touch someone, a result that was hard to measure. More a riot in the heart, then, wherever that was. If we had them here. Maybe Heather had been right, that she had no place reminding people what they had lost.

In any case, the sheet of paper that she had pasted to the span of cork on the second row, middle column, had been replaced with a recruitment poster, advertising employment for some kind of job she didn't understand. The language was vague, expressing an opportunity to work in 'Energy Deployment'. Most of the tickets had been pulled. It was a fact, she realized, that there had been only one outage since the night she had sat with Malor. Maybe after all the city's lumens had gotten the problem under control.

Next to this, in fact on many panes of the carousel, were hand-drawn Wanted posters, sketchy portraits that had replaced the missing persons ads she had seen on her last visit. They bore small descriptions, lamenting the destruction of the station, declaring these people villains. So, it seemed that one of her articles had had an effect. The impression sickened the part of her that held the candle, sending a cold draft across the little flame. She walked away from the carousel steeped in guilt. No, it was deeper, it was shame. So this was how she earned her safety, by making criminals of those who only wished to find their own in leaving the city behind, same as always, perhaps who she'd always been.

The Blurry Mice was situated on the corner of First Street and Pegasus. If there was a sun or moon in Pluto City, the block would have stood in the shadow of the great wall. Instead, it was as sparsely illuminated as any other intersection of the district. Here, the buildings were squat, one or two-story apartments and little fix-it shops and convenience stores. Parked just outside the front door was a long bus, with white paint, sitting on large, thickly-ridged tires. December noticed clods of dust caked into the treads and little piles of the substance gathered on the sidewalk below. She stopped for a moment and appraised it. She had never seen a vehicle of this size, nor had she seen such dust.

Or had she? It reminded her, suddenly, of the long moment that had stretched upon her during the last outage, when her eyes had adjusted to the darkness and revealed at her feet, where the sidewalk had been, a similar material. Had the bus travelled from outside the city wall? Did the evernight extend in some physical sense beyond it? She bent and touched one of the piles, rubbing a modicum between her fingers. Maybe it was only ash. Maybe the bus had only travelled through a neighborhood that had missed its sweeping. A rowdy group of people howled into the night as they jostled into the narrow door of the Blurry Mice, piercing her inquiry. She remembered her appointment.

Why was she even here? Among the school of questions swimming in her, this one felt most urgent. She reached into the boozy memory of her conversation with Heather, grasping for her relationship to the task at hand. To edify a brand new version of the big story, one that treated the very conflict that we ran from as necessary. Essentially good. As sweet as air. Another pail of lies that she would weave into the truth.

Inside, the bar had the same dimensions and organizing concept as the others. Now that she had recognized it, the fact of limited imagination on the part of the designers could not go unnoticed. Or maybe they wanted it this way, to remind us of our sameness, our lack of differentiation, of prospects. The little black tables with their little red-hued imitation candles waving, giving the interior more shadow than it had light. December looked around, saw the same old characters bending to their drinks, the bartender like an installation, with the rolled up-sleeves, polishing a glass. He looked at her with the repetition of curiosity.

"Get you a drink?" he said.

"I'm supposed to see a fight," said December.

"Ah," he said, and flicked his chin to the far end of the room, where there was an anomaly to her eye. A curtained doorway that did not exist in the other haunts. Above it, a hand-painted sign reading "Cosmo's Palace".

She thanked the man and maneuvered around the tables and already she could sense a change in temperature, a heat, an artifact, she thought, in the coding. Something new in this city after all.

The back room was larger than the bar itself, with a taller ceiling, and the floor was strewn with a rendering of Sun Country straw. You could hear it scratching against the concrete floor along with the shifting feet of the Palace's motley occupants. The great room, larger even than Heather's apartment, was stuffed with people. They were all wearing costumes December didn't recognize. Reflective vests over long-sleeve coveralls of a thick material. They were all of them facing an elevated boxing ring that had been constructed in the center of the room, the large flood lamp hung above it the only light, around which the crowd was gathered in a rough circle fifteen or twenty rows deep. Standing room only. There were no seats and so the workers —that was the word that came to mind—stood, shifting their boots on the straw floor, lifting full cups of imitation lager to their lips in between bouts of jeering and laughing, a happy buzz, a tense sort of expectation bubbling out of them, condensing in the air, warming it, strong enough, it seemed, to put pressure on the ceiling, to push it upward, to grow the room in order to accommodate the broad shoulders and ruddy heads and the merriment and vigor they contained.

A sudden hush came over them as a figure emerged from the shadows and climbed a little set of stairs and stepped between the ropes and into the ring. He wore a set of finely-pressed fatigues, starched and squared off at the shoulders. A compact man with a martial bearing, he occupied the center of the ring and stood at a comfortable attention with his hands behind his back, inspecting the occupants of the room until the crowd grew silent.

"Brethren," he began, huskily. A sharp two syllables. "I have been granted the distinct honor of welcoming you all to our fine fighting league's inaugural engagement. If you're in this room, it means your contribution to the city is unmatched in its significance. Believe me when I say that every Plutonian is indebted to your essential service. Without further delay, I would like to introduce the fighters in our main event."

Without moving a muscle below his neck, the speaker looked stage-left, nodded, and the flood lamp above him began to strobe, as a dramatic, epic instrumental track began to play from tinny speakers mounted in the corners of the room. December felt the energy in the room rise as the reflective patches of the workers' vests caught the strobing light, redoubling it.

"Weighing in at one-hundred and eighty-five pounds and fighting out of the black corner, I present to you the Deacon of Darkness, the Prince of Mystery, Kenny Shadow!"

Once again a figure emerged from the corner of the room and climbed the little staircase and stepped onto the canvas, which December noticed now was smudged with crimson. In the strobing light, the fighter's movements were jerky like a film with missing frames. He wore a long, black satin robe and walked with a patrician grace, his chin held high, looking down his nose at the gathered crowd, menacing them as he paced the ring. The crowd booed and hurled insults, spitting mad all of a sudden, as if their response had been rehearsed.

"And now, weighing in at one-hundred and sixty pounds, fighting out of the red corner, I give to you the Matron of Malice, the Sunny Mountain Stone and your people's champ... Mona Kabang!"

The woman who stepped into the ring wore a bright orange robe that bore on its back an embroidered, yellow sun. Her hair was tightly braided against her skull and her jaw seemed to be etched in stone. She moved with a coiled anger, her eyes locked onto the pacing Shadow. The crowd's energy shifted like a stiff wind. It was as though they funneled their energy into her; their intensity channeled into her unrelenting eyes, which focused on their mutual opponent.

To December, it was all a little on-the-nose. The battle between light and dark, Pluto City's classic intrigue, embodied in broad strokes and ladled on the stage. The light returned to normal, casting an even glow onto the canvas. The music stopped and a referee in black and white stepped into the ring. It took December a moment to realize that the speaker and the referee were the same person who had merely changed his outfit.

Now, each fighter retreated to their corners and disrobed. Kenny Shadow, December was surprised to see, was an old man with a fine, rippled musculature and a white goatee. Mona Kabang, the subject of the article she was here to write, had a body that was much younger, had thicker muscles, though she was visibly shorter. She rolled her shoulders. She and Kenny Shadow joined the referee and speaker at the center of the ring. From where December stood at the back of the room, she couldn't hear what the referee said to the two fighters, but each of them nodded and tapped their gloves and a bell dinged and the fight began.

The first round passed uneventfully by December's estimation. It was as though each of the fighters were testing the limits of their relative advantage. The elder fighter was slower yet his strikes were delivered with a technical precision. Mona's movements were inefficient but she displayed a particularly venomous right jab which, just before the bell, connected and opened a thick gash in the meat of Shadow's eyebrow, sending a bloody torrent trickling off his chin. At the sight of the patrician elder's blood, the crowd roared.

The second round began much like the first, with the fighters exchanging an almost polite series of feints and punches, before Kenny Shadow scored a nasty uppercut to Mona's stomach and followed up by grasping her behind the neck with both gloved hands and in one swift movement pulling her face suddenly down. Like a piston, he brought his knee up and smashed her in the face. December heard the nose break as a spray of blood hit the mat. The crowd froze. The referee did nothing. Mona was stunned. She stumbled backward against the ropes and Shadow moved forward to capitalize. However as he reached her, Mona pushed off of the ropes, concentrated her momentum, and swung her forehead into his chin like a trebuchet. The elder man's knees buckled but he stayed up. Mona lifted her leg and struck him in the chest with her heel, the force of which sent him tumbling back into the opposite ropes. As he attempted to regain himself, she clamped the right glove under her left armpit and pulled, freeing the taped fist, the sharp ridge line of her knuckles. Before Shadow had the chance to mount a defense, she closed the distance between them and pummeled him. Again and again with the fierce right jab until he slid to the mat. She didn't stop. She squatted over the creature and further dismantled him, spattering the crowd and soaking the canvas.

When the bell finally rang, the Deacon lay motionless. Mona stood and shook out her fist. It was as though the audience was holding their breath, so that everyone in the room could hear when a rattling, wet moan came from the thing on the mat. Its sharp exhale sent a fine mist of crimson to hang in the air. Without so much as looking toward the elder's body, the referee declared Mona the winner and the crowd was ecstatic.

Just as it seemed the celebrations would reach a fever pitch, more figures emerged from the shadows in the corners of the room. Their costumes were similar to the other workers—they too wore the thick-fabric coveralls—but without the reflective vests. Small medallions hung from their chests. There were four of them and they carried thick staffs and began herding the workers toward the door.

"Show's over! Back to the bus!" they called in unison. And the workers complied. They downed the rest of their beers and looked sheepishly for where to put them. Seeing no refuse containers they dropped them to the floor as they marched past December toward the door. She attempted to speak to one of them, a tall, red-haired man with a thick beard, but he only looked at her, and shook his head as though attempting to forget her, turned his body so as not to touch her, and slid past.

In the ring, Mona knelt to the broken body on the mat. She had taken off her second glove and held a bottle in the hand that had not inflicted damage. The bottle contained a clear substance, like water. She used a portion of it to wash some of the flowing blood from the elders face. Then she lifted his head gingerly and put the bottle to his torn lips so that he might drink. He coughed and sputtered before he took any down. December watched this. December watched as Mona bent to him and whispered something that she could not hear. She watched her slide her arms under the man and lift him. In her arms, the old man looked like a child. She parted the rope with her shoulders and carried him out of the ring, disappearing into the back of the room from whence they came.

# ELEVEN

MONA'S APARTMENT was in the Second District. December had been let in by her assistant and sat in the foyer admiring the wallpaper. It bore a pattern of rich greenery so vivid that it lent the room the humidity of a rainforest.

She felt a certain thrill at the opportunity to do an interview, like a real journalist. She wasn't so much nervous as she was expectant, energized, until the desk in the corner of the foyer insisted on pulling her attention from the rich leaves that seemed to grow from the walls, pulsing with life.

The way the desk's left side leaned against the wall bothered her. It was ruddy, squat, chipped. It should be in some back office, inhabited by petty managers, sneaking from its top drawer lines of cocaine and bags of old potato chips. Sitting at the desk—yes, she found herself sitting at it—the desk felt familiar, too.

For a moment it felt as though she was sitting in the back room of the ticket office where she used to do her homework, as a child, back in the Sun Country. If she listened closely she could almost hear, beneath the night song piped in by the city speakers, the loud chimes and waltzing carnival tunes of the old amusement park in Gracehaven.

August had brought her up amidst its history. She understood it as a relic of a bygone era, built before the roads were paved, when Gracehaven was a budding shipping hub. When the refineries and smelting factories rose up around it, the city center was established to the east, leaving the park to fend for itself amidst the choked steam and rising smoke. But the people of Gracehaven still went and so it stood, the Ferris wheel rising above the squat offices and coiling metal pipes and four-story cisterns of heavy industry.

When the war came, the wheel was damaged by machine gun fire from a strafing aircraft. Though it didn't run, they never tore it down. When the hot war cooled momentarily, the energy rations kept half the bulbs across the park unlit, which gave the park a crooked charm, like a broad smile with chipped teeth. Elders and children alike took the train or bus from the city to toss balls at metal bottles or ride the carousel. Each day after school, December was one such person.

While August finished up his work, she would sit in the back room of that ticket office with a bag of popped corn and her notebooks, mumbling to herself to keep the sounds of the park from interrupting her thoughts. Sometimes, if she finished early, she would ride the zipper or shoot BB guns at paper cutouts of long dead malcontents. Of course, all of the attendants knew her and they would let her have her way. Then August would come and put on a serious face and try to find an error in her homework.

"If you want I can get you a job here right now," he often said, chewing the inside of his cheek in the dim light of the office. "It'd save us the money for the bus fare. But if you want anything more than *this*, keep your head in your studies."

December didn't understand what was so bad about working at the park. She liked what August did, especially when he voiced the puppets. She knew he'd write the scripts, too, often late at night when they returned to their apartment. The audiences were small and she knew they were not rich, but the people who worked the park were kind and the park had free snacks. Still, she heeded his advice. She enjoyed school. Her teachers told her she was smart, that she could one day attend a university for free. She also knew the fear in August's voice, and had a young person's intuition for an elder's crumbling walls. She knew what it was to be unmentionably afraid. She could still make out, at her eye level, the patched bullet holes in the classroom and hallway walls of her school.

She often fell asleep in that back office. The fluorescent bulbs in the ceiling had been deemed too costly, so the only light was from a dim lamp on the desktop, its warm honey hue colluding with the weight of a late night to fold December into the tiny couch in the corner. August would wake her and they would walk together through the stilled and silent park, where only the hum and clanging of the nearby works made a sound. They would coax the cold engine of August's seventh-hand truck through the rigid streets to their housing complex, where they took turns on who got the bed and who got the couch. Oftentimes, when it was August's turn for the bed, he let December sleep there, anyway. So much of August, December thought now, had been carried out as an apology—just like Mona's gesture to the broken man on his back on the mat.

Then, suddenly, the familiarity of her school, of the

amusement park, of Gracehaven's choked skyline and the music of a heaving city had been replaced by a foggy ethereal near-empty landscape. Mirror Bay. What had constituted her sense of home was not perfect, but what replaced it felt like something next to real, a ghost existence. Whenever she asked herself why they left their home in Gracehaven, she couldn't really say. Sure they had a surface reason. Her father's job for the University, but she didn't understand what that meant.

December hadn't lived long enough in the Sun Country to be captured by either of the dueling ideologies. Gracehaven and Mirror Bay had, in her time, been occupied by Technocrats, but she had lived mostly amongst her classmates in school and the people who worked the amusement park, an anachronism that by design was positioned outside of time. The point of it was to escape thinking about the war and August had done his best to insulate her from the current events. It wasn't until he began working for the University, a distinctly Technic undertaking, that any of their philosophy bubbled into her private thoughts. But only barely.

She was sick a lot in those days, beset by headaches, which narrowed her vision to the immediate, the personal acreage of pain where no philosophy took hold. In that sense, she too was outside of time, outside of history, until of course she began helping her father, first in Gracehaven for a short stint, and then in Mirror Bay. But even then, she did not feel the ritual of the transfers they performed to be imbued with any deeper meaning or import; she was simply helping her father with his work. An instrument of history, yes, but not one who subscribed to the litany of belief that formed the choreography.

She didn't even know if her father believed in what he

did. For him, she thought, it was a job. Something you did in exchange for food and shelter. She didn't know what stories he told himself, only the stories he told the people who came to them, which always varied depending on how they presented their reason for being there. If she had him here now, she would ask—how complicit were you, not in deed, but in your thoughts?—but of course she didn't; she had no idea of what became of him, could only guess at what he'd say. To hear the ghosts of words, floating next to the truth, as though we were living next to a life, in a repetition of something that might have never even been.

"December Valence?" came the voice.

The foyer of Mona Kabang's apartment returned to the forefront of her consciousness, and December found that she was sitting on the floor, her back against the rainforest wall, looking up at the boxer, who had a warm—perplexed, but warm—expression on her face. No, there was no desk, no chair. Just the floor and the way a wall meets it at roughly ninety degrees, same as it ever was, here or there.

⸺

THE CEILINGS WERE high and the windows took up most of the street-facing wall. December sat where Mona had indicated, and now watched the woman's movements—supple, but at the same time coiled, piston-like—as she moved to the window and closed it, muffling the night song, and as such the passage of time.

December realized, as Mona stood now, hands resting on the back of the chair that faced her, waiting for her to speak, that she had been given no content brief or direct instructions for how to shape her article about the fighter. She did her best to recall the soggy evening spent with

Heather Mercy, wherein the concept of the fighting league had been introduced, grasping at the words of significance that had passed between them. *Unification, peoples' champion, somebody all of them can get behind.*

"I would offer you something to drink," said Mona, ending the silence between them, "but my kitchen is sort of empty. I've only just moved into this apartment."

"That's no problem," said December. "Thank you for inviting me into your home. It's a fine place."

"Is it? I don't really have much to compare it to."

"Where did you live before?"

A look of consternation came over Mona's face as she looked around the place, as though measuring it.

"I must admit," said Mona, "I'm a bit nervous speaking with you. I've never done an interview before."

December felt similarly, but thought it imprudent to confess her own misgivings. She could feel a nervous kind of tension in Mona's bearing, now that they had gotten down to business. To echo it might put them both off course.

"Well, all I'm really here to do is get to know you, to understand a bit about your story. Why don't you start by telling me where you're from?"

"They told me you'd be coming. Heather... was it Mercy? Yes, Heather Mercy and Jovis prepared me for this conversation, gave me everything I needed, so they said. A profile in *The Pluto City Sun*. That's a newspaper?"

"Something like that, yes," said December, somewhat absently. The name Jovis stood out to her; she'd never heard it before. "Heather Mercy is my editor and I write for them. Did you say Jovis? That's a name I haven't heard before."

"He's been organizing the event and directing the rehearsals."

"Rehearsals?" December asked.

"Forget I said that," said Mona, her nervousness peaking. She walked over to the window and opened it once again. The music of the night song returned. "What is it you want to know? Where I came from, my story?"

Mona returned to the chair and this time sat. A wrinkle formed in the fabric of her pantsuit and she smoothed it. That face of hers, December thought, was like a carved statue of some ornate goddess. Beneath the rippling anxiety, there was a woman of propriety. She half expected double tongues, edged with fire to drop from her mouth each time she opened it to speak. This room, it wasn't good enough; Mona was small, compact, but carried the weight, too, of religions, December thought. She deserved a world.

"We can start anyplace you like," said December. "I was there, in the crowd at your fight. It was really something. You must have put a lot of work into the... would you call it a performance?"

"Please, forget I said anything about a rehearsal. I'm still getting a handle on the language and misspoke."

"I won't print anything you're not comfortable with," said December. "It's just you and me here, sitting together in a room in a city that has been less than consistent as of late. And if I'm honest, this is new for me, too. In fact, this is my first official interview for the paper. I'm nervous, too."

Mona seemed heartened by this. She shifted in her seat, recrossed her legs, now rather than leaning against the side of her chair, inclining her energies toward the window, she was squared now with December, looking at her, chin up a little, a little down her nose.

"You know, I thought it was a little strange when I found you sitting on the floor in my foyer, but then I saw your face. You had this look that reminded me of how I've been feeling lately. You looked stunned, but also like you wanted to laugh. You were stunned and bemused. It was like looking in a mirror lately."

December found herself to be momentarily embarrassed. An aspect of her job that she enjoyed was the perspective it granted on her subjects, but to be on this side of the eyes was uncomfortable. She prided herself on a certain level of flexibility, however, and, reminded of this, settled into the moment.

"My mind has been wandering lately," she ventured. "To places I don't often go."

"Have you been thinking of before?" asked Mona.

"Yes. More or less without consent."

Mona, for the first time, smiled. "Me too," she said, and as she did the smile left her. In fact all the energy in her face fell inward, the eyes settling somewhere deep in a well, far, far away from December's reach.

"My story goes like this. I was born into a family of arms manufacturers and profiteers in the city of Three Notches. A very wealthy bunch, who had taken on the titles of an older sort of gentry. Before I ran away, I had been married off to a rival family, and made a duchess, with all the riches one could ever want. But I was abundantly aware of how these families of which I was a part made their riches, and it burned me up. I hated it. And so I gave it up, and I took my little sister with me, to spare her from the crooked marriage that was sure to eat her up when she came of age. But the route was hard, the fighting far worse than I imagined, and outside Little Apple I lost my sister. She lost her life. And I lost my way. I didn't know who or what I would be, but felt that I would know the correct path when I found it—which landed me on a train to Pluto City. And it was on this train, on the final stretch of my journey, that I met a grubby little boy who had been smoking. He was my sister's age and when the train attendant threatened to kick him off the train, relegating him to the same fate, I believed, as my own sister, I stood up for him and claimed him as my own. And in that gesture, I found myself. I knew that I would find some way to live out that fight in Pluto City, to fight in the name of the little ones who had no one to stand up for them. My guilt over my failure to protect my sister is what gives me a powerful jab."

December was stunned. She recognized the story immediately as that which she had experienced on her way to Pluto City, in her own dream of the train.

"So there you have it," Mona said, sitting forward. "That's my tale."

December didn't want to unsettle Mona, but she noticed most of all that in her telling that there had been no feeling. She sounded vacant. The story felt rehearsed.

"What was your sister's name?" she probed.

Mona let out a nervous laugh.

"You'd think I would know that, wouldn't you? Wouldn't that detail be unforgettable?"

"If this were a normal place, no doubt. But it isn't, is it? Maybe her name will come back to you with the next outage. Memories have been coming back for me ever since they started."

"See, I can't remember a time when they weren't happening. In fact, when I try to remember anything I did in the city before I started up rehearsals, nothing comes. All I have is the story of the duchess, and even that doesn't feel like it's mine. It feels like a story I've been told, as though it happened to someone else."

"I wasn't going to say anything, but when I was transferred here, now years ago, I felt I was on the train, too, living as a duchess. I even saw the little boy you mentioned."

"Really?" Mona said.

"Really," said December. "I took it as a dream, some artifact of another life, another story, that leaked in while I was in between."

"How did you know it wasn't yours?"

December considered this, thinking back to her first night in Pluto City.

"Maybe at first I thought it was, the way you feel when you first wake up from a dream. But I had my memories when I arrived here. Come to think of it, it was only the longer that I stayed here that they began to fade."

"So you had a feeling that it wasn't you. You knew deep down that you were something else."

"Yes, I guess I always did. Even when the big story was at its strongest, when the city had all its light, I had a feeling there was something else beneath it. A sort of ache I carried with me," December said.

"I understand this. The other night, after rehearsal, I was walking through the city, running the story of the train and of the sister through my head, and I came upon this big bulletin board in the center of the district, not far from the hospital where I'd been staying. And I was just perusing it, reading the advertisements, when I found a story someone had anonymously written. It told of a man who had lost his wife and daughter in the war and how he missed them. He had this memory of loving her, in part because of the debates she'd have with the spiders in the shower, and how he'd lay back on their bed and listen and feel this kind of warmth spread over him. And though I knew this story was not about me, it felt so tender and so true, and it made me realize that if I'd really had a sister, I'd have a feeling like that, too. A warm kind of ache, like you say, that reminded me of what had been. I felt a tug in me, yes, but not to anything that I could see. It felt as though I was holding onto a rope that stretched down and down into a deep well, and that on the other end of this rope there was a self of mine that was trapped, that had nothing to do with daughters and duchesses and trains and boxing matches. It made me feel as though I was living in an outline, born just yesterday, as though I was some kind of product, built to do only one thing, to rehearse, to perform, to repeat."

"I know how you feel. The distance is painful," said December, with a mix of sorrow and happiness. That someone had read her article and found an aspect of themselves reflected in it heartened her, but to see its effect on Mona's face now made her question its ultimate effect. A part of her wanted to tell Mona that she had been its author, but she felt unwilling to declare herself as any origin of the woman's sadness, and feared exposure should Mona Kabang divulge this information to Heather or this Jovis.

"I've been questioning the material of my existence, too. What the city means. What I do. And where the lines can be drawn," December ventured, exposing herself. Mona rewarded her with an expression of curiosity, so she went on. "I've also felt like all I've done is lie since I came here, as though that's all there is to tell."

"We need our stories, don't we? I think I understand my role in this. I'll play my part."

"I suppose we do need something to tell ourselves and others. The mind can't bear a gap. That much seems true, whether we're here or in the Sun Country."

Mona was quiet for a moment. She worried again at the wrinkle on her thigh.

"Where'd you come from?" Mona asked.

"I grew up in a town called Gracehaven, a little city in the Middle West."

"It sounds nice to know. For me, everything before is blank," said Mona.

"I'm not sure that it's a blessing to remember what you can no longer hold," said December.

"Of course it is," said Mona, sharply.

"I have to ask," said December. "You've mentioned your rehearsal many times. What did you mean?"

"Well, you can't print any of this, but the fight was choreographed, more like a dance."

"I would have never guessed."

"I suppose that's good," said Mona. "All I've done since I came here was practice for the fight and learn my story."

"There's something I've been wondering about since I watched you in the fight. At the end, after all the violence, when you helped him, was that a part of the choreography?"

"No," said Mona. "That just happened. I don't know how to explain it."

"Ah," said December, smiling. "So that was *you*."

"I guess it was," said Mona, and she smiled too, for a moment. "But I don't know. I don't have any idea who I was, or if I was, only that I'm not that person any longer. You're lucky you remember anything. At least you can see what your tether connects you to, that at the bottom of your well there's something solid."

"We're all from somewhere," December said.

"You sound so certain. I sometimes feel as though I'm a printed object, with no past and no future of my own, as though an ornament is all I'll be."

"You're hardly an ornament. I can tell you that. To me you are a goddess. You'll do things, you'll act on people.

You'll give them something they can use. A reason to believe."

Mona swept her muscled arm across the room, and held her palm to her chest. "I'm not sure I have anything to give if everything in here is hollow."

"Maybe that's okay," said December, quietly.

"I didn't realize you had come to give me therapy," said Mona.

"To be honest with you, I'm not really sure why I'm here. I have an article to write. That's true. But ever since the lights went out I haven't really understood, like what's my point."

"Well you certainly can't print anything I've told you. Stick to the lie."

"I've been hearing that a lot lately. Why is that?" December said.

"Like I said, I'll play my part. I have a story to uphold," said Mona.

"But if it isn't ours, why do we tell it?"

"I've said enough for one night," said Mona, as she stood. "It was nice to speak with you. It really was," and she offered her hand to shake December's. "Remember what I said. Not a word."

December was unsure if Mona had been educated in the physical circumstances of their tenure here, if she knew of its simulated nature. It occurred to her that even she did not fully grasp the quality of this maybe-refuge, maybe-prison. All the same, December felt a rift between them and decided that to tell her anything of the sort would make it wider. She found herself thinking that under different circumstances, they'd have been friends, and wished not to confuse her further.

She wondered later if that's how August had felt with

the clients. He must not have known where he was sending them, having never travelled here himself. Perhaps he felt that they were both caught up in the same ordeal, that any line that separated them was artificial, that they were merely playing their parts together on the same stage. But of whose design?

━━

AFTER LEAVING MONA'S APARTMENT, December walked and sifted through her thoughts. The ash fell softly and caught in the orange glow of the streetlights as snow might, turning slowly in air and settling into a thin carpet on the sidewalk. It had felt good to learn that the freelance article she had written had found an audience in Mona, that the only part of her that felt true had found some kind of resonance. It had felt good to commiserate with someone else who was similarly freighted by the absence of a grounding truth. Though, if she was honest with herself, this had much to do with the possession of her own memories; to meet someone more lost than her made her feel more stable, even if recognizing this came with its own brand of guilt.

She considered the platitude she'd offered. That the hollowness Mona felt inside was okay. It felt now like such an empty thing to say to a person whose identity was so clearly concocted. The train dream Mona had been given as her origin seemed as though it had been written into the code and assigned at random. The only difference between them was that for Mona it had been reinforced as a personal truth, the big story flattening her into an implement of violence, owing her energy to a sister she never had, to a city that cared nothing for the person she had been.

When December returned to her own apartment, she became painfully aware of its size. How small it felt after occupying Mona's. A pang of jealousy rose; how could one so new to the city be given such spacious quarters, while one who had been passing along the city's story for so many years still wallowed in such a humble abode? All the same, the conversation with Mona had made December cherish the memories she held, even if they hurt her. Maybe that was enough to even the score.

In the office, she considered her assignments. There were two that she would write. She owed the *Sun* a column, one that impressed upon the reader the significance of the fighting league and introduced them to the character called Mona. She dispensed with it quickly, typing up from memory the tale of the train and of the profiteers and of the duchess and her sister, this latter thread the righteous motivation for her violence against the representative of the darkness, the old man that she had dismantled on the mat.

The second article, her own, took longer. She first pulled her stack of paper from the bottom drawer of her desk and uncapped her pen. Mona had barred her from publishing the most significant part of their conversation, the expression of confusion that she felt her readers would value most. A fact which irked her. She was already trading away mouthfuls of her self to write the official articles. To be told what not to write in the ones she could control made her feel sterile. Nonetheless, she'd respect the woman's wishes. So then what was left? What were the ingredients she had? What ingredients did she need? What were the elements of a story, anyway? You had to have a source and you had to have a way to witness it, and further a way to impress upon the reader your interpretation of what you'd seen.

December had witnessed the lights going out now, across the city, and with them the very buildings in some places. She had seen the low wattage affect the quality of light in her apartment, and how it seemed that with the ebbing of the city's power, her own memories returned. She had seen the matrons eating people. She had seen at Mona's fight an assembly of workers, a class of whom she was heretofore unaware. Further, she had experienced the limits not only of the city but of a capacity to leave it, the latter of which had been promised, had been a core ingredient of the city's story, the big story that shaped them. And now, she had seen one of the city's newer, braver citizens hiding something. Yes, that much was clear to her as she thought about it now. December had detected a potent reticence in Mona to say much about the orchestrated nature of the fight. And it seemed that whatever it was that was scaring her had her committing to her own version of the lie, even when she did not feel it to be true. Who had that power?

The lumens, of course. They were the only sort of people in this place who had the capacity to make you weigh the consequence of speaking. Who, then, within that context could be her source? If there was anyone she knew who might bestow upon her some rarefied perspective, it was Malor. How well had that gone last time? Putting that aside, she recalled the contours of their previous relations. Throughout their time together, it had always been him summoning her or seeking her out. She couldn't remember a single instance in the six winters they spent together where she had initiated one of their rendezvous. For the first time, the fact struck her as odd. What impulse had relegated her to such passivity?

When the memory came, she snatched its tail with her writing hand and began to sketch quick notes. As the story formed, she felt a feeling rise in her, an unlocking of sorts that reminded her of what Mona had said about her experience reading the article about Szewski. The honesty in her depiction of his tender love had been what reminded her of what Mona might be. December thought perhaps this would suffice as her second freelance posting. She still had questions, yes, that she would address to Malor herself, but for now this might be worth posting. When she finished the piece she lifted the page and read it aloud before making a couple final edits. Then, she donned her coat and stepped into the night, heading first for the carousel to post her story.

# TWELVE

IN THE SUN COUNTRY, the little girl I used to be had few friends. I grew up in the thick smoke of capture and recapture, as city-wide the streets clattered with small arms fire and the redundant, petrifying impact of improvised bombs and whistling mortars. Throughout this time, my father August kept me hidden. It was the two of us always, save when he would go out, pretending a savage limp and poor eyesight, to scrounge for food and candles.

When the Numerals took a resounding hold of Grace-haven, the schools reopened and the children who remained crept slowly back into the halls and classrooms. It took some getting used to. We could always tell where the bullet holes had been patched, the crooked, sometimes star-shaped impressions, always definite in their messaging, lurking, many of them at head height and still lower, come from rifles that had been aimed downward, in the bad old days that were somehow only yesterday.

School took some getting used to. The other children, myself included, were jittery and unaccustomed to such camaraderie that the friendships in those days were delicate in the wind, like new shoots.

When August took the job for the University, I could tell that he was happy. But word spread fast that he was different from the other fathers. He was on the outside now, the other parents said to one another, looking in, and they didn't really much like that, let alone trust him. And so this sentiment passed into the children, my would-be friends, as though it was fed to them, and they were pink with it, and they shunned me and withheld from me their play.

Except for Marcus. He still talked to me. He stood up for me in the lunch line once, and invited me over to play on more than one occasion. He lived in a big house, with big windows and lovely wooden floors and a kitchen full of golden-veined marble that made me feel little in a nice way. Marcus's bedroom had tall ceilings and thick, soft carpet, and he had the best toys and his parents had the best snacks. I always felt good when I was there. To be completely honest, I worshipped Marcus.

Then, one day, we were at recess in the school gymnasium, where there weren't any windows, where it was safe. Marcus and I were sitting on the wooden bleachers, the sort that folded out from the wall in big stacks, like an accordion. Marcus was showing me his new Fighting Angel figurine. And then he dropped it, accidentally. The white and silver Raphael glinted briefly before falling into the dark and out of reach.

I didn't even really think about what I did next. I only wanted to help, so that Marcus knew how grateful I was to be his friend. So, I stomped down off of the bleachers and ran around to the back, where a person of my tiny stature was able to easily walk under the heavy bleachers. Underneath it was like a cave, lit by thin slices of light that slid between the benches overhead.

"Over here! I can see it!" said Marcus, from above, and I followed the sound of his voice and saw the fallen messenger, and crawled on my hands and knees to retrieve it for Marcus.

"1, 2, 3," I heard another voice, and then the wood started to creak and rush toward me. *Whoom whoom whoom,* I can hear it now. I scrambled backward with the accordion bleachers collapsing and cut the palm of my hand on a wicked shard of glass before I got to my feet and ran for the light. I made it out before the children pushed the accordion bleachers totally closed. Their cheeks were flush and they were laughing. Marcus stood with them, steeped in mirth, a double agent, all the while. Worst of all, he didn't seem to want his cherished toy, the one I had risked my life for. The smile left his face only when I approached him and the other laughing boys to present him with the brilliant Raphael, a little dusty from the floor beneath the bleachers, a little bloody from the deep cut in the palm of my hand.

Eventually the cut healed but it turned into a scar, which I carried with me in the meaty portion beneath my left thumb, all the way to Mirror Bay, where there were no schools any more, where there were no other children, save for Milo and for Porsche and for the others whom I briefly met. By then, I had learned not to attach, and to keep the vulnerable, fleshy parts inside of me hidden away. I grew into that distance.

My headaches came on stronger there in Mirror Bay. What had permeated short passages of my waking life invaded me now for days at a time. I couldn't walk; I couldn't read; I couldn't sleep; there would just be the screaming, pumping spasms in my cortex, and the blinding light. For days at a time, my body would turn on me, hold me down, and electrocute me savagely. And the truth was, a part of me was thankful for it. For the body that betrayed me had demands. Satisfying them pleased me, in a way, because it gave me a purpose that was inside, where I was safe from the Sun Country's violent nature. I knew what became of little girls who found themselves alone in the dark.

When I came to Pluto City, I brought with me certain other scars. The headaches stayed behind with the old body, the first body, made of the Sun Country's faulty material. The scar in my hand there does not appear when I look at my palm now. But the effect of this and other cuts, ones carried inside, made the journey. My resistance to exposure stayed on. I kept it as part of my collection of private truths. A spell I had cast on myself to ward off danger and quiet my voice. I learned to speak sideways, always maneuvering around the jagged edges of my private history.

I have for a long time believed that I am soft inside, that ultimately if I allowed my innards to be seen, then the monsters of the world, here or there, would eat them. And the depth of my fear found its bottom and its genesis in the creeping story within me, one I only whispered, that in coming here I had allowed that very thing to happen: that I had been eaten, any significant part of me swallowed by a passionless machine, rendered into lines of ones and zeros. Little electrical impulses, traveling between transistors or whatever it was, pressed into the silicon of microchips that rich men made to keep me, to keep all of us, for their own nourishment, just a feature of their graphs and tables.

But when the lights go out, I feel I'll still be here, the

essential core of me sustained. And I feel that I am filled with it, so that now, as I walk along the faux-real streets of Pluto City, I move like a jungle cat. Fat on the work of my hunt and in no hurry. I have in me my strength and I have my vision. I am strong and I can see in the dark.

# THIRTEEN

AROUND 8ᵀᴴ AND FIGUEROA, halfway down the block, December saw the neon sign for a sandwich shop. At the counter she paid for a rendition of a club on sourdough and the day's paper and sat at one of two scratched up tables in the corner. She hadn't eaten in two days and, now that she was unwrapping the small loaf, realized her waning energy. She allowed herself to savor the first bite and the second, allowing the light that it contained to course through her, livening her mind.

Then, she opened the paper. As she expected, there was no new reasoning given for the outages, only advertisements and propaganda about the problem-people. She skimmed the pages, looking over the headlines for one name. Malor Pendegast. Most of what he'd told her in the paddock had come to pass, so she had to give the rest of it some credence. She remembered what he said, that he was planning to emerge as the city's hero. With the attention ladled onto him after the crash, the iron had been hot for that sort of play. But when she reached the back page, and then scanned through one more time, pausing to finish the sandwich and wipe her greasy fingers on the imitation napkin, she confirmed he wasn't there. So he had maintained the resignation he expressed to her at the bar, choosing the half-self that was quiet. Why?

As she made her way to his building, the lights went out again. Again, the moaning absence. December had learned to simply wait, allowing for the winds of time to pass her. When the lights once again returned, flickering on all at once, the stucco and brick walkup next to her had disappeared. Or rather crumbled. It sat in a silent heap of dropping particles, spreading out like a castle made of sand when the moisture that held it up had gone.

―

ON THE CORNER of Beacon and 3$^{rd}$ was the brick building that housed Tommy's and the antique store with its hand-carved masks and the fortune-teller's window, which had since been repaired. December paid this little mind, the way one does in familiar haunts, and nodded to the two cigarette-burned mannequins with decorated faces as she entered Malor's building.

Once again, there was Gist, with his chiseled body and vacant eyes.

"December V. Good to see you again so soon."

"Is he here?"

Gist jutted his chin at a door at the end of the hall, peopled by the decorated mannequins, and December found the door unlocked.

The studio was large and well-apportioned. The place had a faux-brick wall and big windows. The green fabric of the couch looked Sun Country, rich, and on the tables and kitchen island stood imported lamps, giving the room a low, tungsten glow. Malor Pendegast lay on his back in the couch at the center of the open space, looking up and seeing nothing, though on the ceiling, tiny lights had been set into a satin-black panel, in an arrangement that mimicked a starry sky. She knew this pose. He was screaming high. The jar of glimmer beads open on the kauri table confirmed as much.

"Greetings, sweet prince," she said, using the language of her old entrances, this time with a little salt.

The chemical compound working its way through Malor's simulated bloodstream had enough sparkle for two bodies. He felt himself tipping over the edge of a beautiful vista, swimming really, understanding himself as a billion tingling constellations, an orgasm in constant bloom.

The door opening pierced his kingdom, allowing a movement in the corner of his vision. The shape had spoken. His thoughts fluttered like a thick stack of papers might, if gripped and thumbed at the corner, a word here, there, each grasped for a moment, though leaving, across the pages, meaning stranded. Until finally a string held taut.

"December?" he said, slurring the second consonant. "Oh my god it's you. I've been waiting ages for this moment."

Malor stood and wobbled, balancing himself on the armrest of the couch before wiping a string of drool from his chin.

"The burden of my masterpiece has lifted now," he said. December's pool was still. There was no ripple.

"Sit back down," she said. "I need some answers."

"I'll do whatever you want to do, Ember."

"You don't get to use that name anymore. Now sit."

He did as he was told, or perhaps he had been knocked back onto the couch by the force in December's voice. The couch let up a puff of dust and, surprised by the recent turn of events, Malor rubbed his heavy-lidded eyes and scratched at the thin lawn of stubble at his jaw.

"You sound different," he said.

"The other night you told me the city was breaking, that it was coming to an end," December said. "Despite my thinking to the contrary, it seems that much is true. But the city hasn't seen you. Your story about rising from the ashes, leading, making something of your inheritance. That hasn't come to pass. Instead you're here, wasting away again while the people of the city are scared and confused. Why? Why haven't you followed through?"

"I was wrong. That isn't who I really am. I've been fooling myself. And the story I have to tell, what I know now, is one nobody wants to hear."

"I do, if you can muster. If you can bring yourself to spit it out. If you know something, I need it."

"I thought you didn't want to write my story," said Malor. "I thought you had everything you needed."

"You were right. This is the one worth telling. Not your story, to be clear. You're right to think that nobody would care what you have to say about yourself, your plan for you. Especially now. But what about the city?"

"What about it Ember?"

"That's not my name."

"You can answer questions too, you know," he said.

"Malor they aren't letting anybody leave. That was promised," said December. "A fact I know better than most."

"That's right. Of course you do. You and your beloved father, bringing everybody here."

"Exactly. We told them they could leave whenever they wanted, that this refuge was permanent, but here as an option. This city is a service. Or we thought it was. But now, just like you told me, it seems it's ending and we have nowhere to go. We want our bodies."

"I have nothing for you," said Malor. "Nothing you want to hear."

"Speak, man. Let me be the judge of what I need."

Malor squirmed uncomfortably, as if to burrow in the couch.

"I don't like you when you're like this," he said. "Right now you're very hard to like."

"Don't be a child."

Malor laughed. A little chuckle. He leaned lazily toward the coffee table, reaching for his jar. Before he could touch it, December swiped it and held it out of reach.

"You want this? Then you talk."

"I could hurt you December."

"I'm sure you could."

She walked to one of the large double-windows, swung one open and held the jar over the open air.

"One more bead and I'll tell you all you want to know," said Malor.

"I set the rules here. You talk and then you get your high. I don't want this messing with your thinking more than it already has."

"Fine. You want a story? I'll tell you what I thought I knew."

December plucked one of the iridescent marbles out of the jar. Then she tossed it out the window.

"One down. I'm listening."

"The story I was always keeping from you goes that we are underground. That we are put into physical bodies, that we are still physically connected to the place we left behind. The story is it's a body mill. That sound you hear in the distance, the factory. It isn't a recording; it's really here, built around an ancient tree that was here long before my father and his partner found the evernight. The story goes that this factory is where the products that we use are manufactured, where the bodies we live in are grown. That you are walking around in one now. The story is my father built this city from the ground up, with the aim to get some-place where the bombs couldn't hit him, and make bodies that were cheaper to maintain, that didn't get sick as easily, or addicted. Or hurt. That didn't need as many calories to get the same work done as the old ones. Right, that's the deep truth, that you have to go hunting for. Well it isn't true."

"Well even I know that's bullshit Malor. I know that Pluto City is a simulation. These bodies of ours, these build-ings, even the lights hold no real weight. There wasn't any dying for you in the crash because you're stored on a server, the only piece of you that really matters, same as what was inside the bodies that we transferred, the bodies that we emptied of the people that we sent here. They're the only part of Pluto City that matters, that carries any meaning. And they deserve to know the truth. They aren't customers. Those weren't just clients in Mirror Bay. They were flesh and blood. They were real people. Really what they deserve is to go home."

"That's you, darling," Malor said. "Do you want to know what I think? I think you never figured out how to make a life for yourself. You never made any friends. The whole time we were together, I was the only thing outside your mirror that you ever saw. You picked up pens, you picked up paper, and you put them to good use, but other-wise you never got off the ground. You think the reason that I left you was because of my fucking dad? I left you because I didn't want to live whatever sliver of a life I had tending to you. You're like a creature, you're like a pet, a little house plant to be watered, and you're scared now that your water is going to be turned off. You miss your dad. You always did, and you looked for him in me. You think you're so strong, coming here uninvited giving me shit for how I spend my time. What are you doing that's any better? Why do you think anything you do actually matters?"

The two of them were quiet for a moment.

"Because you need to," Malor went on, his voice sharp. "You need to find a reason to be angry. You need to find a reason to start a fight with anybody you can so you can get any rest from fighting with yourself. That's all you're doing with this little paper. Looking into the mirror and hating yourself and pretending what you're seeing is the city."

December was surprised. Not least of all because he had managed to string together more than two sentences.

"Ever since I can remember, darling, all I've wanted to do is help," she began. "I may have erred when I helped my father, but my father was my only friend. I was a child. I could do no different. I didn't choose, entirely, the things I did. And I'm okay with that. I'm under no illusion that I'm perfect. My hands aren't clean. Even now I'm a little dirty, just like you. We're the same. And yet you sit here, doing nothing, holding the same tools I do and more. I don't care why that's all you're doing. But I am out there, trying to put it right. That's all I'm doing now. It's the only reason I came to see you. But you don't get that. You didn't see the people at the station, terrified. All they wanted to do was leave. We're willing to risk going back to whatever is up there. People like my dad. People like me."

"Please. You're not like them. Your whole existence is built around proving to whoever reads you that you're not. All you ever wanted to be was important. That is not the same as trying to help, to make a difference, or whatever it is you tell yourself to sleep better each night," Malor said. "Now hand me my fucking jar."

December threw it across the room. When it hit the wall of imitation brick, it shattered, spilling the iridescent beads, sending them rolling in all directions along the faux-cement floor.

"Go ahead. Pick them up," December said. "I know you want to. I won't judge. I understand you've got it easy but not easy enough. You. With all your privilege and your influence. The pressure is just too much. But now what you have to understand is that while you may be content to sit back and light the fires and watch the world burn, others are not. That means you have a choice. You can either stand in our way or you can help."

"Our? Who is our? You and your fellow propagandists, calling out the very citizens you mean to tell me you protect? I read the articles, December. I know who you really are, "said Malor. December kept staring into him. She didn't look away.

"Go on," he said. "You mean you're done?"

"You know what I think it is?" said December. "I think you can leave whenever you want. I bet you've got a body waiting for you now, and when this is done you'll just go back. I bet you people only made enough bodies for yourselves, and that's why no-one can leave. Same as it ever was. Just like in the Sun Country when the war started popping off. Anybody with enough money got the fuck out of town or enjoyed the killing from your ivory towers."

"There are no bodies," said Malor. He stood up and collected the nearest bead.

"I know there aren't. I disposed of them myself," she said.

"I'm not talking about the originals; I mean the technic ones you all told them they would get."

"Excuse me?" said December.

Malor dusted off the bead for show and popped it in his mouth. He chewed once to release the juices and let them dissolve under his tongue.

"There are no bodies. Not for me. Not for you. There are no bodies because there is no Sun Country. There was no war. It's all part of the same simulation. The simulation is all there is. The story you tell yourself, the story you think you know, about yourself and where you came from, it was all written by someone else. You didn't live it. You never worked there. All you are is a figment of another mind. And before you get all indignant, and say we're different, we're really not. You and I are both the same kind of real. We're from nowhere December. We're nothing but something that never was. When you really think about it, it's kind of freeing."

The narcotic effects gathered steam and took over his bearing. He sat back down.

"Let's say for a moment that I believe you. Who else knows this? How long have you known?"

"Nobody knows. Except for Jovis and my father. I didn't even know until I..." he looked at his fingers as he used them to count. "Until two nights ago. Father told me, and you have to admit that it makes sense. When you really think about it, doesn't it feel true?"

He was getting sleepy now, head starting to roll. December stepped to him and smacked his face.

"Wake up," said December. She knew how this would go, had seen it plenty of times before. Once the drug got full into its flow he would be gone for several hours. He sputtered up, eyes wide for just a moment, seeing her as if she had just arrived.

"All the time we spent together, I thought I was hiding from you," he said. "I thought I held a precious secret that no one else had. But it wasn't true. None of it was, so I really had nothing to keep from you. We could have really been something. But now that's gone. Squandered, too."

"Who's Jovis?"

"That's a funny question," he said, lolling now. "He wrote the big story. Technically you work for him. My father handled construction. Or so the story used to go."

Malor drifted now, falsely content, eyeballs rolling back and forth beneath their paper lids.

December didn't wait for him to surface. She found the door, and she used it, and when she walked back down the dark hallway, she paid no mind to the crooked mannequins and did not see what stood amongst them, watching.

THE FOX THEATER was on the corner of Weyburn and Broxton. Its spire reached into the evernight sky like a bedazzled arm, the three bold letters arranged vertically, tattooed in alternating blue and yellow neon lights.

December paid and, skipping the concessions in the red-carpeted lobby, padded into theater two and chose a seat in the back row. Ever since leaving Malor's place, the impression of the blood in her had been pulsing at a high frequency. She needed to think.

She had seen this one before. The film told the story of a young insurgent soldier in the Silicon Skirmishes who met the love of his life amidst the final charge of a grand offensive in the rolling hills and valleys of a vast winery. It was well into the second act when December settled into the recliner. She let the images wash over her, the hum and flicker of the projector just audible during the quiet scenes.

The cinema was for her a sort of church, hallowed and grandiloquent in a way that calmed her. She could engage as much as she wanted with the figures on the screen, and as such release her mind. Here, she expanded into her own peaks and valleys. The shadow realms and the areas brightly lit.

If she decided to believe in Malor's story, she would in some sense be free. Bearing no responsibility for the process in Mirror Bay. Absolved of her recent work with Heather. Maybe after all the ache in her was this, knowing, deep into her, that because there was no truth, there were no lies. But in a way, the story Malor told her was all too patent.

That Malor found it out so recently was also suspect. If what he had told her in the paddock before the race was at all true, he had been preparing, in some way, effectively or not, to supplant the city leadership and begin something new. What if his father had perceived this as a threat? If he had, it would give credence to the idea that there was some-thing worth protecting. Some scheme or deeper truth.

Something her own father had said to her came back. The day following Milo's transfer had been quiet. The storm had gone and the sun spilled in through the big windows in the natatorium. They had just finished a transfer when a woman entered. She had been fair of hair and about August's age. Her name was Mora; she said she was Milo's mother. They had lived in the town, the two of them all their lives. She knew about his injury, his severed hand. It had happened on a fishing vessel two days prior. He had gotten it caught in the hard steel gear that pulled the netting. August had apologized to her profusely, and offered her their services. Not knowing whether to treat her like a believer or a skeptic, he toed the line between the two approaches, and all she had said to him was that he had been a liar. She didn't believe his story, and chose to think that they had murdered her only son. She went away, and they had never seen her again.

After the woman left, December had asked him: why didn't she believe you? Why did she call you a liar to your face? He had told her then: in life you have two choices.

"You can believe in God," he said, "or you can believe in a person who pretends that they are God. It's up to you, and up to everyone to choose."

December didn't understand it at the time, though now the credo was a lens through which she saw Malor rather clearly. He had made such a choice long before this night and long before they'd met. He had chosen his father as his God. This choice determined his reality and the role that he would play. In Malor's world, he would always live within the confines of the father. She had abandoned hers, at least in theory. Any freedom she enjoyed relied on that distance. And yet, didn't she still feel requisitioned by August's actions? Bereft of his influence, hadn't she gone looking for it in Malor?

The action on the screen ramped up. Men who looked just alike forming battle lines along their interpretation of the old Sun Country divide, that of faith and reason, rushing over the hills and into bloody valleys, emptying one another of their lives.

Could it be that the source of the fight before her was false? The intermix of light and shadow flashing on the screen not the projection of a real kind of history, but a projection of a projection, pointing back to a core untruth? How did one get outside experience, to really even know? It seemed that if this were possible, it could only come after death, supposing any portion of her substance remained. For the moment, for any foreseeable moments, she could not know. But what felt true to her was this: you needed substance to have shadow. You needed light to have the dark.

Malor's position then, that nothing mattered because everything was false, felt lazy. A rationale for doing nothing. He had chosen to find in a supposed falseness of the environment a falseness of his self, which smacked more of abdication than a version of the truth. Classic Malor, shirking what was his to hold. It was a simulation or it was not. If all she knew was unreal, it still had to have a source. The question then was how to know, by faith or reason, when you had found it.

On the screen before her the battle went quiet. A slow period, a bunker scene between gun blasts. She could hear behind her the flicking shutter of the projector. Where was her source? Was she as near to the picture's source as her own? Or was her projector positioned further away, stretching over time, like the light from a long-dead star, reaching her from some distant and alien past to which she had no essential bond?

The dichotomy she felt inside her was troubling. It mimicked in its own way the warring factions of the Sun Country, her mind caught in a constant and replicating binary, a war over which characterization laid claim to the quality of her essence. She, the propagandist, trapped by shame. Split in two by her responsibility to stay alive and to rectify the lives she'd claimed.

The movie ended and the projector stopped its flickering. As December left the theater and walked into the night, she felt as though she were suspended a little ways outside the city, as though she were floating, yet at the same time connected to it more than she had ever understood herself to be before. If there was anyone following her, she didn't notice.

She looked up at the evernight sky and thought of stars. How long had it been since she saw them? She tried to place them there, tried to impress upon the blankness just one of them to admire, but alas her powers did not extend so far. She listened to the night song, to the recording of the cicadas and to the whisper of the wind between the trees. She missed the forest. She missed the smell of it. Heady, deep, and pungent. The way the sun would fall in great sheets and land in puddles on the carpet of dry needles. The feel of the soil in her palms, the damp, cool mixture, the way she let it slip through her fingers and back to the ground. She had in part lived beautifully in her short time there. She had tasted grapes and mangoes, knew the crunch and greasy pleasure of buttered popcorn. She had known laughter.

December considered the words that Malor had lashed her with, about her bearing in the world and how she had arranged herself. He was not altogether wrong. She had always been angry, gripped by the notion that her life should have been different, that she had been miscast in a world poorly made. She had given this apprehension a certain density that gathered to it so many elements of her person, creating an unfathomable distance between her and other people, between her and her self. Everyone she met had become to her an expression of the wrongness and so she hated them. Hated the poor souls who had come to the natatorium to seek new fate, hating herself for helping them. Even then, she had felt this way. Hadn't she always?

When she remembered the time before Mirror Bay, she

did not detect the same echo of resentment, even after the incident with Marcus. Nor had she been so captured by it in the early days of their work in the natatorium, with Milo and with Porsche. Whatever the source of this all-penetrating woe, she couldn't yet touch it.

December returned to her neighborhood and to the building she called home, floating on the surface of her deeper waters, bothered still with who to be, but grateful that she had thwarted Malor's nihilism. And when she reached the door to her apartment, she found it slightly open, left just ajar, and she felt for a moment as though she had left it that way, like a message of openness to her self. An act of perfect trust. Then she entered and found the note.

# FOURTEEN

WHATEVER HAD BEEN inside December's apartment had turned off all the lights. A primal instinct stopped her and she listened. A wan glow emanated from her writing room and she followed it, tiptoeing through the immensity of silence as though she was the intruder.

On her desk, a candle had been placed. A thin, white, simple candle. The perennial bloom of its flame waving gracefully in the still air. Below it, a folded sheet of creamy vellum, held shut by the candle's small weight and the wax drippings. December felt a chill crawl up from her lower back and between her shoulders and lifted the small faux hairs on the back of her neck. She flipped the switch on the wall and the small room was blessed by the higher wattage of the ceiling bulb. Before she lifted the letter from its place on the desk she went to each room, moving swiftly now, and powered every fixture. Even the living room lamp and the lights above her kitchen sink. She checked the closet. She made sure the door to her apartment was shut tight and locked, a feeble gesture but an important gift to her riled self.

Once she had lit the apartment and removed all its shadows and made sure she was alone, she entered the writing room once more and found the letter and the candle had not been a figment of her imagination. She lifted the candle, and with it the folded paper, and blew it out. When she pulled the two apart, the paper felt heavy and decadent in her hands. It was thicker and richer than any of the communiques that she received through the slot in the wall. She deposited herself on the couch in the living room and read.

> Dear Ms. Valence,
>
> It has come to my attention that we should speak. I have long admired your work and would cherish the opportunity to discuss with you a new role. If you would be so kind as to grace my humble office with your presence, at your earliest convenience, I will tell you more.
>
> Please forgive the nature of this letter's arrival in your capable hands. May it serve only to underline the importance of our work together.
>
> Keenly,
> Jovis

Below this was an address in the First District.

December read the letter several times before allowing it to rest, open, on the cushion next to her. She attempted to absorb its content, to understand what the invitation meant to her.

*Jovis.*

She said the name aloud. A name which only recently she had heard. One of the city's founders, origin of the big story, holder of any answer she could want. He had known where she lived and was aware of the work she'd done. He had violated her home and summoned her to meet him. No, this was not an invitation but a command. One that made her sick to consider, that made the walls of her apartment feel too close, as though the city itself was a room without a door.

She stared at the painting on the wall before her, with its deep reds and pinks, the large foreground with sprays of dark green, and atop the vast red pink and purple ridge, the outline of individual warriors assembled in a line, the beauty before the violence, or before the turning away. A work of possibility; if only she could see their faces; if only she could understand their motivations so that she might be able to diagnose her own.

Twice now she had been accused—by Heather Mercy and by Malor—of wanting influence. That she had comported herself in Pluto City to stand next to power and acquire some amount of it for herself. The accusation did not hurt her because she felt that it was true. What hurt was the absence it exposed.

What had she really ever chosen? When she thought about why she had been with Malor in the first place and why she stayed with him until he left her, she found no point at which she had done any of the choosing. When the assignments came through her slot, she completed them. Even when they felt wrong. When the lights in the city had started to go out and the memories began returning, she had expressed them without clear intention; she merely felt them, took them in her hand, then wrote them down. Always, it seemed, she was merely responding to whichever stimulus had found her. It was as though December was one of Szewski's bulbs. Some thing that either had no energy to conduct or else a broken filament inside. She was an inanimate object, bereft of desire, lacking the capacity to want. Maybe this was what lurked within the shadowy depths of her very center. The ache of knowing there was nothing there.

And yet, there was a pull as though a sail in her, just unfurled, had caught its first lick of wind. Had she, by her own meandering curiosity summoned Jovis, in a way? Whether it was a command or an invitation, the fact remained that the very person behind the big story, behind Pluto City's mask, wished to meet her.

Buoyed by this second interpretation, she stood and paced her apartment. She made herself a cup of tea. She considered the candle on her desk. The trails of dripping wax had dried. The wick was cool and a little of the soot crumbled onto the tips of her fingers, blackening them. She rubbed them together and sniffed them and smelled propriety. She thought about relighting the candle and setting the letter on fire. It would be pleasurable to watch it burn. But she didn't have any matches and the address it contained held for her a potent energy. The thought of losing it needled her. She carried the letter back into her writing room and took a sheet of paper from the bottom drawer and wrote it down, lest the paper it had arrived on were to disappear or break apart.

Could any of the words be trusted? Such compliments deserved a second thought. Or did they? Maybe she had earned them. Maybe she had wanted such attention and the prospect of a new venture. If she was honest with herself, yes: there existed the possibility that Heather and Malor were right, that she had wished with a quiet part of herself for recognition from the city's highest echelon. She, after all, had wished to grow beyond her advertisements.

Perhaps with the quiet part of her hidden in the dark she had dreamed of attaining the perspective of the inner circle and that, with it, she could be strong. True, she had not imagined that it would come this way, by means of forced entry. But nonetheless, she found herself feeling powerful, as though perhaps the letter represented a future she had chosen.

# FIFTEEN

DECEMBER ARRIVED at the dividing line between the
Second and First District, where Coffer Street ran perpen-
dicular to Otter Avenue, along which December had half
expected to find some security cordon, some barrier. It
occurred to her that she might be walking into a trap. The
offer of opportunity that Jovis's letter contained could just
as easily be the premeditation of murder. As much as Pluto
City was an open mouth, full of teeth, and motivated by
hunger, it was an open hand, palm stretched out, offering
fruit. The truth, as she understood it, must be two-faced.
She entered the First District unimpeded.

The quality of the architecture changed immediately.
Where in the rest of the city, the people lived in and
frequented reproductions of this-city streets and that-city
walkups and restaurants and pool halls and tool shops, here
the mansions lay, built of wood and granite, as if felled and
chiseled and joined by masons initiated in a school of
animalistic geometry. The lots on which the buildings stood
were not square, but bowed outward, into the street; there
was no sidewalk, and no choice but to walk in the very

middle of the street, as the buildings loomed and reached outward.

A bear, eight-stories high, frozen in an agitated, fighting stance; its eyes, two windows, lit warmly, were barely visible from where December stood. The wide snout angled a little upward and the detail of its fur was articulated finely, the texture amply defined by the other carved windows set into its stomach, soft semi-circles, six of them, that glinted with the same warm light, and gave the impression of spear wounds.

There was the low, long home in the shape of a jaguar, poised and ready, chin to the ground, waiting for a morsel, its fleshy nose adorned with a finely woven metal handle, the door bearing two portholes for nostrils.

A spider, too, a gaudily big tarantula, with thick legs. December imagined, inside of their tips, little bedrooms and nooks, and from them hallways lined with small, framed pictures, and little ladders that gave way to steps, and then the gradual walk into the sumptuous abdomen, the central room, where an old couple smoked in private comfort.

She had to learn to see the addresses, which were buried in each building's context, emblazoned on a tooth, or a necklace, or a splint. Human forms, too, were memorialized in the occasional six or seven-story residence. And it was quiet, as though here the city was hungry for sound, too, even though it was already fat on melody. Here, the night song did not play.

When she came to the planet, eight stories wide, and eight stories tall, decorated by clouds and continents in carved relief, she found Jovis's address on a plaque that hung on a thick chain, worn round the neck of the muscled Atlas who hunched over, his chin a mere six feet from the ground, freighted as he was, totally, by the weight of a sculpted World. The figure's arms stretched back, and in the shoulder, there was a window, where someone was watching her.

December felt a chill. The silhouette slipped away from the window before December could make any associations.

From where she stood on the street, she heard the front door to the mansion open. A solid groan. In the doorway, framed by a warm tungsten glow, stood the boy who had been watching her from the window. She thought she recognized him. The angular shape of his face. His broad nose. The boy stood, his own shoulders curled a little forward, the head inclined with a forced servility.

"Ms. Valence?" came the voice, which sounded older than she expected. She was surprised by its timbre. And as she moved forth, underneath Atlas's neck chain and toward the entrance to the mansion, she was surprised as well by how tall the boy was—there was something about his bearing that was childlike and diminutive, and yet he stood a head taller. And there it was again, this sense that she knew him from somewhere. She offered her hand, and noticed that both of his were intact.

"Call me December," she said. He seemed nervous to take it, but when he did there was a warmth and courtesy to his touch.

"Welcome. The house is glad to have you."

"Likewise," she said. "What's your name?"

Perhaps he was an automation and the familiarity she felt was due to his replication of the standard text. No, that wasn't it. Automations were bland and effective, but they had no affect. If personality were a scent, they gave off nothing. No, this boy was like her in a way. She felt he had a wide open space in him, a private galaxy, and there floating in the air between them, the tiny particles of a common history. She felt she knew him, the way you know a path in a wide open field of summer-dry grass, firmly trodden, routine, the way a breath is, a comfort here.

"Maximum," he said. "Max."

And with that he turned and led her into the stone foyer, into the world-weary sculpture's stooped frame. The floor was a hard and polished marble, or so it seemed. She was overcome by its grandeur. A tall ceiling, the hollowed-out head of the carrier above, with a large, warm fixture dangling in the empty cranium. Maximum led her up a set of stairs, at the top of which were two short hallways, one into each of the shoulders, from whence the boy had watched her. He looked back at her then, the soft features of his face—when had she known him?

"This way," he said. "Master's waiting."

December noticed the thickness of the carpet beneath her feet, lining the long hallway that he led her down, which was decorated by realist oils of wartime cataclysm, hung at intervals between delicate, fire-lit sconces, their quality vulgar and imposing. A hallowed hall, lit just enough to impress upon you its owner's worth. Music, strings and horns, a symphony, spilled quietly from an upper floor.

At the end of the hall, they came to the double-doors of a gilded elevator. Maximum led her in, and pressed a button, one of four, in the burnished wall, and the double-doors closed silently, well-oiled and patient. The two bodies stood closer now; she felt a heat. She searched his face in the vague reflection of the elevator doors and tried again to place him.

"Have you always been called Max?" she asked.

The elevator doors slid open before he answered.

The music was louder now, the instruments giving way

to a roaring baritone, an opera voice, and again the thick, plush carpet greeted each of her steps as though to usher in a final sleep, the comfort wooing. Max led her out of a small chamber and into what must have been the center of the mansion, where a rotund banister of varnished oak encircled a great volume of open air. She placed her hand on the thick material and looked down; a story below, a vast garden, tropical, almost humid, with green vines and lush leaves, and flowers so bright it was as though they too sang, a symphony of life and brightness, planted in terracotta pots, lit by an impossibly large bulb, hung two floors above.

"We really must be moving on," Max said, reminding her of his presence and again of her own presence here inside the planet mansion of the man called Jovis, whose name had been scrawled in perfect ink at the bottom of the letter that spelled her doom or her liberation, or maybe both.

Down another hall they walked. The opera grew louder, the voice belting in a language she did not know, from another country, a foreign time. At the end of the hall, a set of double-doors, thick and stately, with brass handles and iridescent, deep-blue paint, layered so as to give its own sense of light.

Max lifted the knuckles of his right hand and knocked exactly twice. December felt as though she were suspended, a little ways outside the city, somewhere else, inside herself, and the doors opened, and there he was, the man called Jovis. The music stopped.

It was as though he was composed of a different material than the rest of them in Pluto City. The particles more alive, the mountain of his frame, ponderous and corpulent, held lightly all the same, carried more detail, more lines in the face, greater expression.

Jovis stood in the library at a generous drafting table, on which had been constructed a scale replica of the city, as a conductor might a podium; his arms had been crossed, you could tell, and when she entered and he saw her, he stretched them out and faced her, in welcome. He wore a collared shirt, a tie, polished shoes, and fitted trousers. His face was old, his hands were bigger than they had any right to be, and it was as though all he was was movement, punctuated by a fiery set of eyes in an ancient-looking face. The contrast stoned her. She hadn't seen anybody rendered in such detail since the Sun Country, and she realized in a fleeting instant how little and anonymous she felt in her smooth, mass-manufactured body. The music had stopped and she realized he had been singing, singing over the city from where he stood, weaving its mysteries, its spells and the cadence of its tale.

"Ms. Valence! You have come! Come, sit with me. You are right on time."

Jovis ushered her toward two deep chairs, set facing each other at an angle before an ornate, now dormant, fireplace. He waited for her to take her seat. She was numb, a little woozy, and found she sat, as instructed, and then he took his own, and when he pointed at the grate with one of the massive hands, he summoned thick and luscious flames and a sense of warmth washed over her. It felt so real. So painfully real, and the pain of recognition, of what was here and what was there, what she had lost, snapped her back into her faculties. Here she was, sitting at the roiling center of the big story, with the shadowy figure she had been working quietly to circumvent.

"I am thrilled that you have accepted my invitation," Jovis said demurely, as though he was making a confession.

"Considering the nature of your delivery, I wasn't sure I had the freedom to decline."

"Whatever do you mean?"

"Well you did break into my home. Some might call that domineering."

Jovis looked bemused.

"I'm curious," he said, words dripping with a syrupy kindness. "What gave you the impression that the apartment belonged to you?"

"I've lived there for many winters. It's where I sleep and work. I earn it every day."

"Now, let's not confuse ownership with occupation. It will only make it harder for us to understand each other."

"Fair enough," said December. "Why *did* you send for me?"

"Straight to the point. I would expect nothing less from such an elegant instrument. To put it plainly, I have been following you for some time. I'm an admirer of your work. You have established a potent credibility with our readers. By reminding them of what they've lost, you've introduced them to the possibility of a new life, which happens to dove-tail nicely with our new project."

"I was only carrying out the assignments I was given. It's Heather who deserves the praise," said December.

"Ah, Ms. Mercy. If I may be candid, her editorial regime has proven ineffective. No, I don't mean the official articles you carried out at her behest. It's the tone of your little free-lance articles that I'm after, your anonymous postings at the carousel."

December's face must have betrayed her shock. Suddenly she felt naked, exposed.

"You seem surprised," he said and chuckled. "You can't honestly think I would not monitor the public boards. The story we tell here in Pluto City is my realm, and I pride myself on keeping abreast of all its voices. Don't worry. My intention is not to punish you. In fact, just the opposite. I'd like to offer you a promotion, should you find yourself prepared to accept a greater responsibility."

Jovis was watching her with a sort of hunger when a familiar *ding* came from a speaker in the wall.

"Maximum," he said, breaking his gaze and motioning vaguely to where the boy, December realized, had been standing in the shadows. "Check my inbox. If it's Schulze's piece, slate it for publication in tomorrow's rag, page two, below the fold."

As Max carried out his instruction and left the room, December collected herself. So she had been found out, yet contrary to a fear she had not put words to, she had not been swallowed up by matrons. This, for now, was good enough. When Jovis settled his gaze on her once more, she forced a calm into her bearing.

"The work, as I'm sure you know, it never stops," he said. "Where was I?"

"You knew what I was writing all along."

"Yes! And the humanity you showcased is very useful to us. Truth be told, you were not designed as such and may have rightly been dismantled, but miracles abound. We have a way to bring you under our umbrella."

"And what's this project? Can you tell me more?" December said, chilled by the ease of Jovis's threat.

"But of course. I am nothing if not transparent. You will have noticed our little issue with the lights?"

Of course she had. She said as much. Then Jovis stood and spoke.

"For all the time I've spent here, the night itself has been our enemy. Our fight against the darkness and all it represents have been the very animation of our culture. And for so long we didn't need any stories of what we left behind. Only loose reminders of the war, you know, to keep us thankful for this refuge. Well as it so happens, we're rather reliant on the war above to keep us going. A fact we discovered somewhat late. And as we have witnessed, the proceedings in the Sun Country have somewhat cooled. So, it has become abundantly obvious that for us to sustain our tenure here, we need to sort of... reignite the conflict. And to that end, we have our project."

"You want me to help you start a war?"

"War is all there is, December. It's only a matter of choosing sides. The people who came here did so to avoid that choice. Unfortunately, there is a percentage of every population, in every war, that for all the good and righteous reasons to fight choose not to. The young, the old, the weak, the physically disabled. This city has always been a way to train them up, to make them want what they should have in the first place. To fight. You have already played a significant role in preparing them for this responsibility. You need only complete the gesture, and I am only too happy to offer you the opportunity."

"And what if I say no?"

"You won't," said Jovis. He was looking at her now, standing next to the replica of the city. "I know your story. Who you came from. Your father's dedication was the source of the dispensation that allowed for your access to the stature you enjoy and any capacity you have to understand with some precision who you are and where you came from. Not everyone who calls Pluto City home is single-origin, like you. Some here were conjured up and created from a mixture of the raw essence you and your father, and those like you, harvested at stations across the Sun Country.

Like Maximum, a melange of several souls. You have been rewarded in ways you can't begin to understand for your contribution.

But I don't make a habit of giving gifts to those who don't have it in them to return the favor. What I'm offering you is akin to partnership. A truly unique opportunity. You've always danced around the outskirts of the inner circle. This is your chance to join us at the center, at the very source of the power that shapes the world for so many."

December recognized the pitch. It reminded her of something her father would have said as part of his presentation to a potential client. She wondered then if Jovis had been behind the materials they had used, the pamphlets and the motivational credos. Had Jovis crafted them, and as such crafted important aspects of her own trajectory? If so, then the story of Pluto City had reached beyond the limits of its immediate projection, the streets and city lights, the buildings and the people that lived amongst them, as though the simulation had permeated her life, made her subject, made her contingent, even before she reached it.

"What I'm offering you," he said, reaching into the silence of her consideration, "is the opportunity to shape lives. To shape history."

"I don't know that that's anything I've had my sights on. I'm more interested in giving people the tools to shape their own."

"Don't be silly. Of course it's what you wanted. Otherwise you wouldn't have gone out of your way to post your little articles. You know, just as I do, that if you want to shape your own life, you must shape others' lives around you. To that end, you must recognize who you have a claim of power over—that's life's great game—to understand where your leverage lies and apply pressure to the lives you have at your command.

This life is not a question of giving gifts, of giving tools, as you say; it's one of developing advantages through mutual benefit, and capitalizing on them. You've played a good game getting my attention, and you have before you a new bit of leverage, a new advantage, and now it's up to you what to do with it. I know what I would do. Of course each of us is unique and has free will. But she who helps the powerful extracts some of that surplus power for herself, and realizes the experience of gain. That is life's great game, the only one worth playing."

And here, Jovis had exposed to her his theory. Of course, to him, this life of ours was just a game. A yielding to the impulse of numbers, a life measured and quantified, the soul drawn and quartered, given over to the zero sum expression of winner and loser, of sheep and shepherd. Life a sport, the scoreboard following you as you woke and slept, flattening day and night and all the scents and music it contained into the flip of curving numbers, the call of the announcer in your head, applying stories to the random numbers generated by the seconds of your life—this, the game, this life, a game. Here was the simulation creeping in, squeezing her throat; this was what had haunted her, what she breathed in every breath and what she ran from, what she looked at now, sitting here, appreciating Jovis's decadent frame, the feeling of his carpet beneath her feet. The evidence of this power, of Jovis's and the world's, the power of history—a collection of small exploits totaling up to the amassment of great privilege—was hard to deny. In this room, now, his words felt true, and it nearly crushed her.

"I'll help you on one condition," said December, willing a steadiness into her voice, wanting only to leave with whatever remained of her self and any information she could take with her.

"Very well," he smiled. Jovis appreciated a wager. " You'll do well in life, thinking like that."

"Answer me this question."

He gestured his assent.

"The evernight, the city, is any of it real, or is it all a simulation?"

"Ah, the question at the very center of the maelstrom. The evernight was here before myself and Mr. Pendegast arrived. You could say, relative to our little city, it is tangible. Close as you can get to a corporeal place. A kin of Hades and the like, a place existing in the back of every mind. Our city, though, is rather different. A projection, a little game, made up of the memories we hold."

"So the material of the city, what you built it from, is memories."

"Indeed, Ms. Valence. Such is why the story that we tell is so important. And now, for my condition," he said.

December reeled inside, but nodded.

"Your freelance articles must stop. It's unbecoming of your new station. That is, assuming you agree to join us."

"Yes," she said, unsure of what she meant. "I'll help you."

"You'll help yourself," he said and clapped his hands. "How wonderful it is to be correct in choosing sides, no? Maximum! Enter!"

He must have been waiting, just outside the door, because the strange boy entered, diminutive as he had earlier been. In the light of the fire and in the ample light of the large office, she nearly recognized him. He was someone she had known, and something more.

"Send a note to Pendegast. We'll need to adjust Ms.

Valence's housing arrangement. Something in the Second District, something ample, maybe you-know-who's," and Max bowed, "and bring us some of the good champagne. I'd say we have a good reason to toast our little miracle, our little city in the dark."

Once the champagne had arrived and been poured in crystal flutes for both of them and once Max had left them once again, December spoke into the silence that had bloomed in Jovis's comfort.

"What's your story?" she asked. "What were you doing during the war?"

Jovis turned inward, but he did not let on. "My story is unimportant."

"Well you clearly know something about mine," December said, and he was beginning to grow annoyed with her. He had said his piece and she said hers, and now it was time for her to obey him. Nothing else. "It seems only fair for me to get to know a thing or two about my new friend."

Jovis thought, when you are a child, you believe in fairness. The idea consumes you and nothing hurts more than unfairness. When you become an adult, and maybe this was the most important marker for the transition, you understand that fairness was the fairytale, that the real world cares nothing for you, that it will murder you and feel nothing, that it will thoughtlessly anoint some of us to do its killing for it. The adult human understands this, that life is simple, that it comes down to one simple equation. Chaos cannot be mastered; it must be fed. And what we sell the children who still hold on to fairness is the illusion of cause and effect, something graspable and fair. We sell order to those who never managed to to leave the childish thinking behind. And all the tools they had before them turned to ash in their hands before Pluto City was even a twinkle in his eye. He did not share even a sliver of this thinking. He did not share how he'd been feeling lately, since the lights had begun to go, that there was a balance, that in the end all the scores were settled.

"That conversation," he said. "Is for another time. Here, drink your champagne. You don't want it to get warm. In two nights time, we'll have a proper banquet. You'll meet everyone. It shall be grand."

December drank her glass and later, when Max led her to the door, the emptiness had found her once again and settled in her bones. Max seemed to sense this.

"He's not as powerful as you think," he said. "It's only when you believe his story that he becomes so. Trust me, I would know."

## SIXTEEN

DECEMBER'S new apartment in the Second District was just as she remembered it. The great mirror hung, just as it had before, expanding the already opulent dimensions of the open living room and kitchen that had, last time she crossed the landing, belonged to Heather Mercy. This must be a mistake, she thought, and called out Heather's name. Of course, there was no response. Despite her sense of impropriety, December stepped inside.

Her painting had been installed above the fireplace. She found her clothing had been deposited in a corner of the bedroom closet, one that was large enough to walk inside of, to contain a chest of drawers. The bathroom floor was marble. It contained a clawfoot tub. The office was as large as her last apartment. On the desk sat her typing machine. Next to it, a note in Jovis's hand. All it said was *Welcome home.*

She searched everywhere for signs of Heather, in the drawers and in the cabinets, and found only one, a solitary bottle cap to her favorite liquor, left behind in the bottom of the trash.

She realized how little she knew about the woman, how little she had even asked. What she had wanted for herself, what she had planned for, who she had been before she came to Pluto City was a mystery that now, somehow, felt out of reach. To be thinking of the woman in past-tense chilled December, as though by remembering her this way, at the same time hollow and impermeable, she created a kind of ghost that watched her now and whispered to her in a language she couldn't parse.

So this was the reward for her compliance. To be copied and pasted into a life that wasn't hers. She felt as though she had been crudely written, privy only to the thoughts she had been given, laden now with yet another heavy truth. She felt she should be happy to have learned about the organic nature of the evernight and the possibility of a return to the Sun Country, but the apprehension was tinged with something else. A feeling that the properties of simulation had less to do with a physical environ, which was malleable and escapable, but of a deeper nature, occurring inevitably at her center, like a cancer in the bone, carried with her everywhere, a part of every act.

December returned to the office. She picked up the note once more from where it lay next to the typing machine. *Welcome home.* Was this her culmination? When she commanded her little simulated fingers to type out letters, what separated her from this machine? How much variation was there when she herself felt instrumentalized, made object, meant to repeat, repeat, repeat? She too felt hollow. She too felt like a ghost. A sorry husk, a mere reflection of an illusory hope.

In the kitchen, she dropped the letter in the trash to join the forgotten bottle cap. If there was a home for her, this wasn't it, this grand apartment, haunted by her flattened selves and Heather Mercy.

She hit the street in search of nourishment. The day song played its midday melody. The ash fell lightly. The sidewalks of the Second District were of the same material as the Third, but swept more often, so that her footsteps left no prints. She was hungry. Gilda's was close but wouldn't do. Too reminiscent of theft, too fancy.

December ventured back into the Third District, past her old neighborhood, to the very outskirts of the city, as far as she could get from its center, from the concentration of its voice. She walked past person after person, each of which also walked alone, possessing furtive eyes and wired jaws to match her own.

In Pluto City, no one ever really talked to one another. The lines of communication had somewhere been cut, perhaps mirroring the enforced disconnection between a person and her past. This was what was missing, the essential piece, this understanding of individual context. The big story, come to replace what before would have anchored a person to her time and place, tethering her instead to a hollow framework that held no room for her experience, her potential and her hopes.

This, she realized, was what she had attempted to redress with her articles, the ones that mattered to her, an energy which had ultimately been absorbed into the body of the very master she sought to contradict.

As she crossed the intersection of $28^{th}$ and Maxim, the sound of people speaking lifted from the road before her like a beacon. Her hunger grew. She followed it and found, tucked out of sight in a tight back alley, an unmarked door. There were no windows. The light inside was low and warm, provided by the wax candles that sat flickering on the two long tables, each with a bench on either side, adorned with plates and bottles of wine. The scent of meat and onion and golden pastry mingled with the music of conversation as the people at the tables carried on. December couldn't tell if it was a restaurant or the living room of a private residence; it was both homey and communal; the people gathered here could have been customers or members of an extended family, or both. A woman sitting at the far end of one of the tables caught her eye. There was something familiar in her bearing. She sat forward, her chin cupped in her palm, listening, until she noticed December and the two locked eyes with an almost imperceptible glimmer of mutual recognition.

"Welcome in," the woman said, standing. "Sit anywhere you like."

December was used to occupying a table of her own, but here, that option was not available. She was suddenly timid, sheepish-feeling. Where she stood, she was on view, and so found the only open space, at the corner of the table where the woman had been sitting, and settled into it reluctantly. The group at the table barely acknowledged her at first, preferring to continue their conversation. December felt the bench beneath her, edging toward its end. The man next to her wore a beard and corded sweater. He turned to her and smiled.

"It's a long winter we are having. Good to be someplace warm," he said. "I'm Salvo, this is Petrie and Moreau."

She introduced herself and waved, and as they returned to their conversation, December watched the familiar woman as she strode to a wooden cabinet set against the wall and pulled from it a fresh glass and a plate and sat it in front of her. The way she moved, with a self-assured grace and straight back, reminiscent of something. A jungle cat, perhaps. As the woman plucked one of the bottles from the table and poured up December's glass with a rich wine that turned ruby in the candlelight, she spoke.

"How many would you like?"

"I'm sorry?" December said.

"Pasties. It's what we serve. You are hungry, no?"

"What's a pasty?"

"It's a savory pastry filled with meat and vegetables. Of the people who settled in the little town where I was born, a large portion of them came to the Sun Country from Cornwall. This is their regional dish. Similar to an empanada if you've had that. A food of the people. My little ode to the old world. The kitchen's closed but I can warm some for you."

December was struck by the ease with which the woman pulled from her own memory, and by the cadence of her voice, as though she'd heard the woman speak before.

"Sounds delicious," December said.

"Most people start with two."

"Well then I'll start with two."

The woman disappeared through a door in the back. December idled, taking in the room. She noticed on the wall there were some of the Wanted posters hung, only they bore doodles, little mustaches and goatees and horns drawn in red ink. One of them depicted the man sitting next to her, this Salvo.

"Do you find it looks like me?" he said, having caught her making the comparison. December sipped her wine, feeling a pang of guilt that her very work had motivated the original disparagement. Had she endangered this very person, and every other person in this room? But his voice was kind and his bearing comfortable; she did not sense a worry or investigative inquiry in his tone.

"When did you have the horns removed?" December asked.

"They're under here somewhere," he said, smiling. She found she enjoyed this repartee.

"Well that's just it!" the man named Petrie bellowed from the other side of the table. "You never could get past the blockade that time of year, even when the guards were sleeping. They had those damn autonomous searchlights with the cameras always looking. The wall here looks just the same."

"I certainly wouldn't try it," said Moreau.

"Well that's because you're a coward," said Petrie, playfully jeering the other man. "Isn't that right, Salvo? Isn't Moreau a bit of a coward?"

"Oh, sure. Moreau's quite the coward, so long as he's got Gurna waiting for him at home."

"True, true, only a coward abandons love, so in that case I suppose he's quite alright," said Petrie, his eyes gleaming with drink and mirth. "Why didn't you bring her along? This room could benefit from a little beauty," and then his eyes fell on December. "A little more beauty, I should say."

Normally she resented this type of comment. She had no choice in her container, so to have it complimented meant less than nothing, feeling instead that it was a question of power transference, giving the beholder a sort of license to the body it hadn't earned. But the words had been delivered without a leering element, and so made her feel as though she was welcome in the room, a part of this motley group, sitting down for dinner in a warm room in the depths of the Third District, as though these were her friends.

"Where'd you come from?" Moreau said.

"I'm staying in the Second District at the moment. But I lived here in the Third for many years, mostly all my time here," she said, feeling slightly embarrassed about the locale of the new apartment, as though by staying there she was violating the newly established bond.

"Second District. Wow," said Petrie. "We've practically got a lumen in our midst."

"Oh, stop it," said Moreau. "The city's all the same. I mean in the Sun Country. Where are you from?"

The woman returned with a basket of warm pasties and put two on December's plate.

"Anybody else hungry?" she said.

"I'll take one more!" the voice came from the other table, while Moreau, Petrie and Salvo were looking at December.

"I grew up in Gracehaven," December said.

"I know Gracehaven," said Moreau. "Heavy city in the Ohio region. Techno stronghold. Real fucked there at the start of the war. We've got a survivor on our hands," he said, and the men at the table raised their glasses and took a solemn sip.

"Not the most accurate renaming, it must be said," spoke Petrie.

"God the names are stupid," agreed Moreau. "Is that where you ported in?"

"Anybody else?" the woman's voice was now behind her. This time Petrie piped up and lifted his plate and the woman tended to it from the basket of steaming pastry.

"Well, no," December said. "After Gracehaven, my father and I moved to Mirror Bay. That's where I transferred."

"Thank you, Porsche," Petrie said, and a wave of shock rolled over December.

"I know Mirror Bay," said Porsche, who now stood still, with that straight back, looking at December. "A little seaside village. Yes, there was a transfer station there. The machine was in a great big pool house. In fact, the machine was built into the bottom of the empty pool. There was a man there, and a little girl, and together they worked the station. The generator was spent when I arrived, so they took me in and fed me and offered me their couch for the night. But I couldn't sleep. I knew it was my last night in the Sun Country, so I sat up and watched the candles burn, and the little girl, she watched me from the top of the stairs," she said, speaking loud enough for the room to hear but never pulling her eyes away from December. "I knew there was something about you that I recognized. Something in your eyes. You're her, aren't you?"

December realized that every face in the room was turned toward her, waiting to hear what she might say, waiting to see how Porsche would judge her.

"I am, yes. Or I was. That was me," December said, feeling the walls close in around her.

"Well isn't that something," Porsche said, flatly. December suddenly felt as though she might be exiled from the room, the truth of her complicity laid out for all to see.

"I didn't understand what we were doing. I'm sorry if I hurt you," December said.

And for a long moment, Porsche looked at her, and the room was silent.

"Hurt me how?" Porsche said, setting the basket on the table and crossing her arms.

"By sending you to a city that broke its promises, that wasn't ever what we said that it would be."

"Oh, please. You think *you* sent me here? Darling, my decisions brought me to Pluto City. Without them I wouldn't have all this, or know these people. It's rude to suggest that any of that belongs to you."

"Here, here!" said Moreau.

"What was it like working at the station?" said Petrie. "Did you enjoy it?"

"What happened to our bodies?" called a woman from the other table.

"Stop it. This woman is my guest, not the subject for an interview," said Porsche.

"Well we ought to know! She ought to tell us!" the woman stood.

December's imitation heart beat faster.

"Like it or not, all of you chose to come here. Were we misled? Yes, the argument can be made. But remember how bad it got. Can you confidently say that, with all the information that you now hold, that you wouldn't have made the same decision? Knowing everything I do now, I would. I can't speak for any of you but I won't let you attack the girl. She must have been twelve last time I saw her. You can't hold her accountable for the weight of the world then. Just as you can't blame yourself for what you did before you came here. Pluto City is a new page in a new story. All that matters is what you've done since," said Porsche. She was incensed. Her chest heaving.

"Well, what have you done since?" asked Salvo.

"Yeah, little Second District girl? Who'd you kill to get that placement?" said Petrie.

"Enough! Out. All of you. You clearly can't behave," said Porsche. "I mean it, kitchen's closed, the wine's gone empty. Come back tomorrow if you'd like. We won't make anything of ourselves if we tear the real people around us apart."

It was the guests' turn to look sheepish. They did as Porsche told them and stood, gathering their coats, finishing their wine, taking last bites of the pasties on their plates. December stood, too.

"Not you," she pointed at December. "You and I have more to discuss."

ONCE THE RESTAURANT had cleared out, December and Porsche sat across from one another at the end of one of the long photocopied tables, alone but for the candles and the faces on the Wanted posters, flickering in and out of shadow, a bottle of wine and two glasses between them.

"Thank you," said December. "I don't feel that I deserve your defending me, but I appreciate it all the same."

"I created this place on the very outskirts of the city for a reason, so that people could come here and get away from all the bullshit, to have a meal, to sit together, trade stories, to listen and laugh. I stood up for you because they were coming at the conversation all wrong. Here, you get to choose when and if you tell your story. Nobody's allowed to take it out of you. You looked uncomfortable, so I shut them down."

"I can't tell you how much it means to me," said December.

"Forget about it. It's done," said Porsche as she refilled December's glass. "What do you do now? Tell me about yourself."

The sensation of the wine was different from Heather's liquor; it caused an inward opening rather than a sublimation of one half.

"I write for the paper," December said. "For the *Pluto City Sun*, in all its wisdom, trotting out little bullshit columns. I'm the reason those Wanted ads went up. I tried to do a little freelancing on the side, to tell the sort of stories that people would see themselves in when they read, but I'm not sure it did anything but make it worse for people in the end."

Porsche refilled her own glass and took a drink. December watched her weigh her words, not with malice but with care.

"A propagandist with a broken heart. Your father must be proud," said Porsche.

"I wouldn't know. I haven't seen him since Mirror Bay, since the night of my own transfer. I don't even know if he's alive."

Porsche considered this.

"Sooner or later we are all abandoned by the people we thought would be there to protect us. In that sense, we're all orphans," said Porsche.

"So you believe we are alone?"

"Lonely maybe in the way we feel, but not alone," said Porsche. "I think we're connected by this feeling. Together we make each other whole."

"But what if you hurt the people around you? What right do I have to safety? I mean, I'm grateful for you defending me earlier, but they ought to know their lives were stolen and that I helped."

"I know how you feel. In my past life, I helped destroy a lot of lives, and I spent a lot of time feeling guilty for it. Still do sometimes. I'm a part of why so many people wanted to escape the only home they knew. Forgiveness is a fickle beast, especially when you're asking her to carry such a load."

"Do you ever wish you could forget it all, just live as a blank slate? Free of any thoughts and any blame?" December said.

"Before I came here, sure. To be honest with you, there

was a time when I thought the only way to make it right was to end my life. I felt like I didn't deserve the air I breathed. Around the time I decided to try the transfer, it was this or that. But then I asked myself why I did what I had done. When you're in a fight like I was, you don't kill for yourself. You kill for the people fighting next to you. You kill to keep them alive. And you follow orders. We were fighting other warriors. Back then, it was only people on the other side of an ideology that contradicted mine. And I decided that was my mistake, taking onboard the story that I'd been given, forgetting about my own. Coming here was an extension of that thinking, a reaching for the parts of me that had been broken off. I told myself that this was another chapter in a new story, that for once I would write. But, no, to answer your question, my life wouldn't have any meaning if I cut myself off from the things I'd done, what the scared little girl in me thought she had to do to live the right kind of life."

Porsche reached across the table and held December's hand.

"Whatever you do next belongs to you," said Porsche. "No matter how hard they try to take it from you, your life is yours."


TO BE REMEMBERED, to be seen and placed in the world. To be warmly touched. It struck December forcefully. She left that evening full of light, a cool orb inside her shimmering, like the full moon reflected on the surface of an ocean.

# SEVENTEEN

DECEMBER FOUND herself standing on the cool cement of the pool decking. She wasn't wearing any shoes. The pads of her feet were cold and her father wasn't with her. She was alone in the natatorium and it was a sunny, clear day. The water in the bay was a patient blue and the gray gunship was close on the horizon, belching its diesel cloud.

She had by now accrued a deep mistrust of August's business. She felt a certain anger toward her father and so this morning had walked out in front of him. When she heard the metal natatorium door squeak open, she resolved to keep her eyes on the sea and not to greet him.

"So there she is" the voice was not her father's. December turned.

Silhouetted in the entrance, for just a moment before the door shut behind him, was a broad figure. His long hair was soaking wet and water clung in beads to his lengthy, silvered beard. He wore no shirt. His trousers were of simple linen. Tattoos read across his rumbled musculature like the thin lines of a short novel. When the man pulled his eyes from the machine where it was settled in the deep end of the empty pool, and settled them on December, he wore a deep and hearty smile, and in that smile, and in this countenance, December felt the sudden breath of an open window.

"So you are the master of the machine?" he said in a bemused tone. The man's voice was deep but not unkind.

The man moved on the balls of his feet and though thickly built moved lightly. When he arrived where December stood with her back to the window, who stood still and breathless, he offered his hand.

"Featherweight," he said, and his sinewy hand was cold in December's small grip. "It is a pleasure to finally meet you."

Up close, looking up at him, she saw a face etched and weathered, brown hair giving way to a regal silver, chopped in places as if by hand with a single blade. The eyes glimmered in their shallow wells.

"Why are you all wet?" said December.

Featherweight jutted his chin toward the gunship on the horizon.

"It is a dirty vessel, but did its work in carrying me within swimming distance. The currents were generous to me."

He left December's orbit and approached the edge of the pool, plodding with his bare feet, leaving puddles on the gray cement.

"Don't use it. Nobody knows where it actually goes," said December. She had felt as though she could trust the man, and found, suddenly, that she cared for him deeply.

The door to the natatorium squeaked open once more as August entered and, seeing the stranger, took into his eyes the salesman's gleam.

"Welcome," he said. And Featherweight turned and offered his hand in kind.

"You look as though you've had some trials," said August.

Featherweight, looking back at the machine, once more, was a man transfixed. "Maybe she is a little smaller. But all the same, she has a presence. Your assistant has advised me not to go."

"Has she?" said August, and found December stably avoiding his gaze. She was looking at the man, who was older than August by many years, for whom she felt a protectiveness bloom.

"It isn't good," she said. "The machine will eat you. Ask my dad where it goes. I bet he can't tell you."

Featherweight's grin was incandescent.

"I have been on my way to this moment with you fine people for more years than either of you have been alive. I left the evernight, now, so long ago, it seems, yet really but an instant, and then another instant more. Always my home has been just on the other side of a steady count. For years and years I have been following the quiet breath of a dream, gathering stories and impressions of a wide and terrible and wonderful world, and now it's time for my return. You see, my people, they live in a solid place, without sun or moon or stars. Stories nourish them."

August opened his briefcase and pulled out his pamphlet, smudged still by Milo's blood, now a deep brown hue.

"Does this place look familiar?"

Featherweight breathed heat into his fists before taking the laminated sheets of paper. He flipped quickly through them before handing them back.

"A fine city, indeed, but it isn't mine."

"I'm afraid," said August, "I only have coordinates for this place."

"I'm more interested in what holds it," Featherweight said.

"Can't you just go home the way you came?" sputtered December.

Featherweight smiled then, his wild and crooked smile, and showed to August the inside of his forearm, where tattooed in fine black ink were a series of points and numbers

"They came to me," he said, "in a series of three dreams, each stanza hidden in the strangest of places. The last? The point-two-four? I found it inscribed on the back of the devil's eyelid."

August compared them to the coordinates on the pamphlet and found they matched.

"Why can't you just go home the way you came?" December had said, louder now. Her voice echoing off the faraway ceiling and returning, quickly doubled.

Featherweight leveled onto her his patient gaze.

"In my culture it is frowned upon to return to a place by the same route that one left it. When I left my home I was just a boy, not much older than you, fair girl. Each winter is time for each able minded person to perform a quest, based on the most potent dream one has over the summer. No matter what occurs in that dream, if we see an item, we must go and find it, if we see a mountain, we must go and find it, no matter how far it takes you, no matter how long it takes to find. For me, it was a ship, with an evil inside of it. This took me many years to find."

The man named Featherweight seemed to drift away into a sumptuous memory. With a smile on his face as though he had tasted something delicious, he arranged his body in the chair and leaned his head back on the rest.

"I don't understand," said August. "The machine was built here only a year ago. How could you have known?"

"I always knew that I'd return, but of course I had to wait for my dreams to tell me where to go. Sometimes I would go two, three years, without a message. But over time, after all, they came." He looked to both of them then. "The challenge in this life is to trust and to have patience, and to learn to do with little. Without this treasure, the world will swallow you before your time."

How could this man, after so long on the path, trust their operation? How could her father send this man to the unknown fate of the others? How could he do this? A quotient of the particles inside of December had then rearranged around a central point, as though pupils to the firelight, reminded at once of the essential story. Behind her, she could almost hear the clicking together of stilled conscience. This moment, this man; this was why she had come here. To save him from himself was the true nature of her role.

"December, will you please ready the power source?"

She didn't move.

"December, now!"

Despite the warning in her cells, she complied, and as she did so, August readied the syringe.

"Save it for your next passenger," said Featherweight. "This body and I have come to an understanding. The poison you hold there will dull the both of us for the journey, and I need as much of me as possible to make it to my people. What I carry must arrive untainted."

"Very well," said August, and strapped his body harder to the chair.

Energy came into the machine. August input Feather-weight's coordinates. The coordinates for Pluto City.

All the while, December buzzed with a confusing mix of love and anger, even while she carried out the command August had given her.

"You're going to feel a heavy pinch and then, well, hold on, alright?" August said.

Featherweight smiled. "You were a part of my dream, you know. You're the one I was supposed to find. I met a traveler some time ago. She had your kind of sadness, and I think it was she who brought you to me. I saw you here. I saw this portal. I knew you'd send me to my home, and send me safely."

Here came the sacred moment.

August breathed and lifted the hose from its holster on the side of the chair. He breathed and separated the body from its essence in his mind. He focused on an area of tanned skin between the fifth and sixth vertebrae, and ran the longest of the two tensile rods downward through the spinal column. The second found its home snuggly in the base of the body's skull. Featherweight was inside himself now, humming slightly.

August nodded to December. She tried to resist. Every instinct in her had told her not to, but she pressed the button to begin the cycle, and felt immediate regret. So as the hoses filled with an iridescent and beautiful orange liquid, she felt a furious pressure in her building.

And she went numb.

As the automatic process carried on, transfusing the storyteller's essence, December, standing next to the machine, lifted her arm. The hand, which worked like a separate person now, gripped the hose where it connected to the machine itself. The hand gripped it and it tugged. It tugged the hose out of the machine and the pressure that had built in the hose sent Featherweight's orange hue spraying across the cold gray cement.

"December!"

August snatched it from her and plugged it back into the machine. But the pressure was all wrong. The liquid began coagulating where the hose met the machine, and darkening, as if molding.

"December why!"

Once Featherweight was emptied, the machine clicked and hummed, and carried out the transfer of what was left, of what had made it into the tanks. The rest of Featherweight lay in small puddles on the floor, losing hue, quickly drying into sticky, colorless nothing.

December was frozen, eyes wide at the puddles on the floor. Realization dawning on her, booming into the matter of her like waves across the shore.


ALL THERE WAS to do was bury it. On account of the gunship the sea was too dangerous for their normal method. They returned to the big house on Chief Street and remained there long enough to run a clean bed sheet through the dryer, warming it. December carried it numbly to the natatorium in her backpack.

As the sun tipped gingerly behind a rolling bank of fog, they carried Featherweight's body to the golden rolling hills and found at the base of the great wall, smelling strongly of creosote, the remains of a majestic black oak. At the base of the oak's trunk, December chipped at the dirt with a little spade, helping August dig a grave.

Afterward, they sat a while. The wind picked up and tugged at the black oak's spreading crown, branches reaching out like bolts of stilled lightning. The zinc-colored sea stretched out quietly below.

"Why'd we come here?" asked December. "Why'd we have to leave Gracehaven?"

After a while, August spoke.

"Why did you do it?"

December nervously reorganized a patch of loose dirt with her toe. She didn't know.

"Maybe he's okay. Maybe the most important parts of him made it," she said.

August put his arm around her shoulder but offered her no words.

The town below was still. Nothing seemed to move.

## EIGHTEEN

DECEMBER HADN'T HAD an answer for August when he asked her why she interrupted the transfer. She hadn't known then why she pulled the hose. All she could feel was her father foreclose on her. He had been wary of her after. She could feel the pressure of his mistrust, of his hatred. And so the hate she felt from him turned inward. And two nights later, the storm had come, and the klaxon rang, and she was gone. Off to Pluto City on her own.

She found, now, as she floated in the tailored car that Jovis had sent for her, above Hope, that great boulevard that stretched between the Central Library and the Hospital, that she had believed in Featherweight. Upon meeting him, she had chosen him as God. And she had hated him for trusting them. For allowing the beauty of his story to be consumed. She wanted to stop it. She had felt so ultimately powerless. She had wanted to save him. She had wanted to save herself. She had wanted to hurt her father. She had wanted to sabotage their work. And she had failed. For even this she blamed herself, the little girl who she had been.

Located in this memory, which she had avoided for so

long, was the wellspring of her constant ache. She felt suddenly relieved of this, enough to see the message that she now needed, that none of this was her fault. She had been captured by a false equation, made to feel that her essential gesture was to take these hands of hers and pull the life away from prophets. She had been chasing false ones ever since.

And so, a lovely tear emerged in the stitching that held the fabric of December's story and the fabric of the big story into one piece. She felt she had something of her own, that she, in fact, was her own. It was as though suddenly the membrane between her and others dissipated or burst somehow. She wanted to know and be known. The feeling of aboveness left her. The coronation of her woe was interrupted. She felt as though she was free of it, of the essential separation that had been eating her.

Cosmo's Palace, the new arena, was being built in the center of the Second District. The walls and buttresses, the giant courtyard before it, all but the dome had been completed. When the car landed, the door floated open like a wing being lifted. She stepped out. The paving stones that comprised the Palace's courtyard gleamed in the night, catching particles of the golden-hued lamps, as though the stones had just been watered.

The entrance was between two great colonnades. Two matrons standing guard recognized her. She was welcome here, and so she walked past them without incident. They nodded to her in a stately manner, their impassive, slightly smiling faces dipping forward as she passed them.

Chandeliers hung in the lobby. The floors were polished marble. She could hear voices coming from the second floor. She walked across the lobby and stuck her nose into the atrium, where the ring was being constructed. A light rain of ash fell through the open dome.

She followed the voices, up a plush red-carpeted staircase that wound around and eventually deposited her in a long sort of foyer, or almost ballroom, just off the luxury box seating reserved for the lumens. And there they were, the lumens.

Jovis was here. She recognized two others. Everyone was dressed finely and the conversation bubbling out of them was peppery and sharp. Controlled laughter and quiet commiseration. The peak of fineness between them. If only they knew the plan that she hid behind her acquiescent eyes.

She recognized the martial type, the general-esque persona who had introduced and somewhat refereed Mona's fight. He had swapped his army fatigues for a three-piece suit and stood with a looser bearing, talking with another finely dressed man, laughing. Pointing upward.

Then she saw it. December hadn't registered her at first, had taken in the shape peripherally, as another chandelier, which in one way was true. Hanging in the center of the room from a rope tied round her neck was Heather's body. The face was blue, the neck broken, the body hanging limply, threaded with string lights.

December froze.

"Ms. Valence! The woman of the hour has arrived!" called Jovis from across the room.

The room's rarefied occupants turned to her as one and smiled and greeted her. An attendant floated over to her and offered a tray of fine champagne flutes. She allowed herself another glance at Heather's body, reading in its pose a clear and present threat. *This could be you.* It emboldened her, reminding her why she was here. She plucked a flute from the tray and held it aloft.

"Allow me to propose a toast," continued Jovis. "To our new member, without whom we would not reach our ultimate success. I'm coining her the Voice of Freedom. She has cracked one of our most supreme challenges, and I cannot wait to see what she does in her new position as our Director of Communications. I give you Ms. December Valence. Here's to freedom!"

"To freedom!" said the chorus of lumens who were gathered in the hall.

"She has more or less been with us since she was child, starting out in the transfer stations in both Gracehaven and Mirror Bay, and continuing her labor for the force of truth here in the city, and asking nothing in return. She is a true lumen, and I request you all treat her as such. She has inherited an instrumental role in surmounting our current challenges, and over the coming season, I encourage all of you to get to know her better, as I have."

December was immune to the charm. She was here to collect her evidence and suggest a second meeting. For her plan to work, she needed time.

"Thank you for the introduction, Jovis," she said, taking an air of propriety into her voice. "I look forward to working with each and every one of you as we further the interests of our grand refuge."

"Here, here! To refuge!"

"Your father would be proud to see you now!" said a man she didn't recognize, who wore a grizzled beard and stood on the outskirts of the gathering.

"Friends and associates, shall we begin."

In the center of the room, below the Heather-chandelier, was a rectangular table and as Jovis took his seat, so did the others. December followed suit.

"Mr. Schulze, would you like to start us off with a perspective on business development?"

"With pleasure," said the martial character in the three-piece suit. He stood and walked to the wall, where December noticed there was a large frame covered by a drapery. He pulled the drapery off to reveal, taking up a large swath of the wall, a map of the Sun Country.

"Our present focus is on the formerly contiguous United States. Scouting reports paint a picture of a less-ening demand for military engagement, which as we know is severely impacting our operations here. What we're chiefly working on is a two-year plan that sees us emerging in the country with a fighting force of 5,278. Now while that may not sound like a lot, the legacy belligerents are atrophied and diffuse. There are one or two robust contin-gents in the Ohio Territory and a security force assembled in California, where our main node is located, and where we plan to make our first incursion. Our goal in business development is to attack, recruit, re-mind. It's our belief that we can attract a good deal of new investment, such that we can get our production lines on the surface back in order, so that in five years time we have enough fighting units for every soul in Pluto City, with a high-level number at give-or-take 20,000."

"Very good," said Jovis. "Let's hear from Product. Ms. Pendegast, do you have something to present?"

December hadn't noticed her before. Olivia Pendegast, Malor's mother, wore a lithe artist's body with delicate, strongly veined hands. She stood gracefully and moved to the head of the table. Her presentation style was such that she walked back and forth as she spoke.

"Let me also say, since we're all here to give congratulations, that your work in quickly revising the matrons was nothing short of a miracle."

"Thank you for saying so, Jovis. It was some of my proudest work," said Olivia. "Allow me to commend you and everyone in this room for working so hard to ready the public for the coming release. We're emerging from the design phase with a lovely selection of new products."

She floated toward the map and peeled back the sheet that held it to reveal an illustration of six weapons. A machete, a pistol, a rifle, a long and wicked knife, along with a small truncheon and a grenade, each in its own box, organized in a sort of grid.

"With Ms. Valence's help, we hope to push these to the catalog within the week, to get people thinking about how they might use them. I believe this will put us on pace to meet the two-year plan Mr. Schulze outlined. The objective here is to furnish our public with the tools of business that they would most recognize from their time on land. For many who have spent significant time here, it will take some reminding of how precisely to use them—our pre-release of one was a little early—which we'll need to be careful and deliberate in trotting out. But I have all the faith in the world that we'll get these into the right hands along with the correct instructions. Allow me to just say that I'm more than thrilled to bring about this new season for our city."

"Here, here!" said Jovis. He was clearly quite impressed.

Finished with her speech, Olivia took her seat.

"With that, let's hear from finance," said Jovis.

The hulking man with the grizzled beard stood. He stayed near the table, and spoke a little awkwardly, not so used to speaking in such a setting, December could tell.

"As you all know, the slowing of the war has had a significant impact on energy production, but we've got ahead of it now. Doubling shifts with the help of Ms. Pendegast's infusion of workers, such that I'm confident we'll be able to support the city and the necessary transfers for another season. We have enough energy stockpiled to meet production quotas for these new objects as well. But I suggest we continue the program of rolling blackouts in the Third District primarily. I know this poses a risk of recall within the population, but I think with a concerted effort from Ms. Valence in comms we can continue to tell the necessary stories to instill the necessary motivation amidst the reorganization of energy distribution."

He sat down quickly, having finished his spiel.

"Ms. Valence, do you have anything to add at this time?" Jovis said.

While she was nearly bowled over by the flood of information, December expected the address. Clearly everyone gathered here had had time to put together a presentation, her lack of which would be her advantage.

"I agree with everything that has been said. I'll need a little time to absorb this, but I think we're well-situated to support the effort here," she said.

"Very well," said Jovis. "Now, let's wrap it up with sales, shall we?"

A little, cramped man stood and he motioned to the corner of the room. The attendant who had carried the tray of champagne flutes emerged from the shadow at the corner of the room, pushing a large, wheeled cart.

"Right here is good," said the little man. "No, no. I'll pull the sheet."

And when the little man pulled the sheet that covered

up the tray's hulking object, he revealed a scale replica of Pluto City's Third District.

"Ladies and gentlemen, friends and colleagues old and new," he began, slowly. Taking in the room, looking each and every person in the eyes. Even December. Even Heather. "It's so good to see us all in one place after the difficult winter we've all had. I believe now more than ever in the inevitability of our success. To that end, I present to you the tactical implementation of your various stratagems. The tip of the spear, so to speak. What we have here is the Third District; you'll note certain buildings and apartments are highlighted in red. These designate the problem-people we have selected. If we're to have our citizens ready for a surface incursion, they'll need to be reminded how to use the lovely tools you, Olivia, will be creating.

What I propose is a door-to-door approach, beginning first with these unsavory individuals. Thanks to your good work in communications, there exists a natural animus for them, so I really don't think it will be very hard to arm a certain contingent—we'll need to work on who—and put to use, in the tradition of a real guerrilla war, these tools. In this sense, we'll reacquaint the users with the sound of gunfire, the feel of flesh on the blade, and remind those on the receiving end what it meant to fear for their lives. Basically, this reintroduction of the essential fear will, I believe, produce a useful defensive and offensive posture, and ready both for what will need to be done on the Sun Country when we arrive in two season's time."

A silence fell across the table as the lumens considered the pitch. So the veil had been lifted, December thought. This was what they meant to make her party to. An entrepreneurial endeavor interested in the exchange of lives for power. And her role was to distill this into purpose, same as it always was.

Jovis cleared his throat. "I imagine you plan to inflict on the bodies a certain damage. So long as we'll have the energy to reprint them, I say it's fine. We don't want to fully dismantle anyone. We'll need them in one piece for the incursion, after all."

The ruddy, bearded individual spoke up. "Maurice and I have spoken privately about this plan. I've budgeted the energy cost for repairing the bodies. So long as we have a focused approach, we'll meet our quotas."

"Yes indeed," said Maurice. "And since we'll not have the bodies for everyone at first, we don't need every Plutonian healed in time. If any of them are too badly damaged for quick repair, we can consider them for later movements."

"Very well," said Jovis, nodding. "We can think of it as a training function, both for victim and aggressor."

"Precisely," said Maurice. "The old dichotomy, as it were."

"December," said Jovis. "How are you feeling about all of this? Have you anything to add?"

Frankly, she was horrified, but she calmed herself by imagining what the people of the city would think once they had heard it.

"It's a good plan, a lot to absorb. I think that we would benefit from having a carefully plotted communication plan, which I look forward to putting together. May I suggest a follow-up meeting, in two nights time? Having heard your presentations, I'd like an opportunity to shape up my own. At which point, I'd be thrilled to move forward."

"Of course," Jovis seemed satisfied. "Same place in two

nights time?" The others nodded their assent. Except for Olivia, who kept looking at her. This woman, Malor's mother, was staring at her like she was hungry.

"Then I'd say the working portion of our gathering is done. What's say we dine?"

"I'm not satisfied," said Olivia. "Jovis I understand you have experience with this specimen, but to the rest of us she is an unknown quantity. I'd like to hear what the young woman has to say for herself."

So she was a stranger to her, December thought. Either Malor had never mentioned her name, or the woman had forgotten her. She realized that forgetting was a key ingredient in Pluto City's makeup.

"You're asking these people to kill and die to carry out your work. On that subject, Maurice, they're already afraid; conducting raids door to door is going to wreck them. Going to wreck any part of them capable of building whatever world you think you have in store."

"Excuse me?" Maurice stood. "I—"

"Let's not allow this to become unproductive," Jovis said. "The reason Ms. Valence has been invited in is she understands the contours of the people's interior lives. What they believe about themselves is crucial to impressing on them the correct narrative."

"Narrative narrative narrative," said Olivia. "You've always thought this is the most important thing. But it isn't. If my husband were here he would tell you: your stories do not matter. The world is made of acts and objects. You make of people objects and you tell them how to act. It's orders that matter, not the stories you form around them."

"And as always we disagree. But this isn't a conversation for this setting. Ms. Valence has much value to bring to our operation, and that is that."

"Well I certainly won't be dining," Olivia said, and stood, and promptly walked out of the room.

December didn't hide her smile.

Anxious to return to some sense of polite engagement, the martial man in the three-piece suit said some kind of joke and the table laughed and soon enough they were all congregating around the trough of food that December wouldn't eat.

■—■

WHEN SHE RETURNED to the apartment in the Second District, she stood and looked at herself in the big mirror in the hall. There was the body. The body of an adult. The one she had lived in since she arrived here. Itself, made of particles of light, pixels maybe. She couldn't know. Her two eyes, nose, the mouth, capable of speaking. She looked at her hands, scrutinized their material, wondered at their ability to cause and to affect.

December made a fist of her right hand and punched the mirror. She wanted to know if it would hurt her and it did. Signals fired someplace in her, carrying warning, the facsimile of pain, as quickly as the material of the mirror broke and spidered outward. Tiny bits of the reflective glass fell to the floor and made a twinkling sound. Imitation blood streaked down her wrist and in the material of her knuckles, two shards of the mirror poked outward.

December plucked them and dropped them onto the floor next to their brethren. In the kitchen, she found a towel and wrapped her fist. Normal as anything, an injury like any other, here or there. You never felt the damage, only the chemical and electrical rendering of its effect. The realization calmed her. She found it wholesome and complete.

In the writing room, she observed her keyboard. It was set into the desk, and held a little spool of paper, on which the words of her reporting populated when she typed. She sat into the chair. The sensation of its support was so familiar. It reflected the certainty that she felt. She allowed the knowingness to hold her, and within it felt the outline of her self. She felt its contours, invisible, draped in shadow, holding shape. She spread her hands out on the desk's hard top, the bandaged one and the one uncut. She realized she was not a chair. She was not a keyboard. She had capacity. She was not inert.

If the city was made of memories, and the big story was what wove them together, holding them in place, then the threat she posed was in returning the very substance of the city to people it belonged to. That was what the lumens stood against, and why Jovis had moved to absorb her efforts into his project. This project to coalesce a people's memories around a new war, not only to collect our pasts, but to control our futures, to allocate us as resources in a self-serving design, to seed their immortality. A maladaptive response to their own fear of darkness, the fear of death, written into the big story, into the code, killing us to save themselves.

What could a life, free of these false parameters, contain? Who could we be? New questions found utterance, echoing off the walls of the quiet place in her, newly found. On the night that she had traced the rail line to the limits of the city, why had she stopped? She had believed then that nothing could exist beyond the influence of the lights. She felt now that she had been wrong. When the city failed, we would go on. Some part of us remained organic.

This was what she'd write. The story she understood, beginning with the outage. She'd write for Milo and for

Featherweight, for Heather's past and Mona's future. She'd write for herself, the little her who had no voice, who didn't have the ears to hear her self. She'd name the story for her journey.

For two nights, December wrote, fingers bleeding through the makeshift bandage on her writing hand, her mirror hand, leaving drops and smudges of crimson. She wrote everything that had happened up to now, including all the details of her conversation with Jovis and the revelations of the banquet, to disseminate what had been hidden and relegate the relationship she had had with Pluto City to ink and dust, to let them know that she remembered and that she held them and that she knew the possibility you contained. For want of a city we had made one. We made it worth understanding and being in. The city was made of you and made for you, its buildings and its streets, the whole circumference made to fit into the palm of your able hand, and still more beyond it, the inheritance of your private history. Let the lights fail and the city crumble. After all, you will still be here, inside of us, inside of you, all of us carrying each other, damn the light and damn the dark, they mean nothing without your love.

━━━

DECEMBER WAS WRITING the title on the top sheet of the draft when she heard the footsteps. She hid it quickly in the bottom drawer. Just in time for Jovis to enter and lean against the frame. He was a big man, corpulent and grand, but his power lessened here. He looked to December like the cartoon of a bear in a tuxedo. The claws softened by the artist. The rounded features making him dull.

"What has happened to your hand?" he said.

"The mirror made the room seem too large. I was uncomfortable. I think I am not used to such expansive quarters just yet," December said, and he softened even more, believing innately in her smallness.

This was her advantage.

"There, there. We'll have you fixed right up after the meeting," he said, moving further into the room, to stand over her where she sat. "I hope you don't mind I let myself in."

"Oh, not at all, what's mine is yours."

"I'm happy to hear you say that. Shall we be going then? I cannot wait to get to work"

"I'm nearly finished here," she said. "Why don't you go ahead and I'll come along."

"What did you think of my little name for at the banquet? The Voice of Freedom. Doesn't it sound nice?"

"I think it's grand," said December.

Jovis began to pace around the room, moving his arms like a conductor.

"Of course your official title is Director of Communications, but I thought something with a little panache, a *nom de guerre*, if you will, would be nice."

"I think it's lovely," she said, "but I really must insist on finishing up my presentation. How about I meet you there?"

"Have you written something? May I see?"

"I haven't got it down on paper yet, but I've done the thinking."

He leaned against the wall and crossed his arms.

"Well let me hear what you've got so far."

December improvised.

"Well, my first thought is, we shouldn't phrase the movement to the Sun Country as returning. The policy of forgetting has been effective in impressing on the people the importance of the city as *the* entity to care about, but what you're proposing would benefit from a proper valuation of the future. An open field, so to speak, is more attractive than an unmarked graveyard, even if the two plots of land look the same. So, I would say, we tell a story that positions the Sun Country as an altogether new place. Give it a new name. Make the people think it is their future they are building, instead of a reclamation of a certain past you've chosen for them, that was lost, that you'd like to have back."

"I'm not sure that's advantageous," said Jovis. "To give them a section of the future that isn't theirs to have. All I see that accomplishing is discontent which, as we all know, is expensive to address. Ms. Valence, haven't you ever wondered why there is no crime in Pluto City? Why you, a young woman, can walk the streets and feel confident you won't be molested? It's because the citizens here feel that they are hiding, that they are wounded, maybe mortally, and must recover before they return to hunting form. The injured wolf doesn't chase after its quarry. It licks its wounds. It waits to be strong once more. Pluto City, by design, is this waiting. A necessary depression in the wicked abundance of the human's normal faculty. Your role in this is significant. You should be proud of your contribution. You should not be attempting to shoot it up with holes. For as long as we operate against a common enemy, peace itself, we are all safe. You are safe."

"Well, it sounds like I should do a little more thinking," said December.

"Perhaps you should, but don't take too long. Shall I send a car?"

"I'd be pleased to walk," said December. "If you think I'll have enough time."

"We'll wait for you to get started," he said. "Remember,

the citizens are not really people. They gave up that distinction when they chose to come here. They are agents of our design. You'd do well to keep that in mind."

"Of course. I'll be right along."

A night ago, she would have been angry. Or worse, depressed by her contingency. But she felt no connection to the man's words. She was confident he would fail.

What she did instead was send a message, using the typing machine and slot in the wall, addressed to Jovis's residence, from which he would be away for a useful amount of time. She remembered Max, what he had told her at the door, how he had been tasked with Jovis's inbox.

*Max, you said the other night that he is not so powerful. I'm inclined to agree. I have a favor to ask if you will hear me out. Wire me back if you receive. December V.*

December waited in the office until her own inbox *dinged*. A sheet of paper spooled out.

*Yes* was his reply.

He signed it *Milo*.

## NINETEEN

THE DRAFT of December's manuscript was too thick to keep in the pockets of her trench coat. She had to carry it in her arms. She knew that she was visible. She knew she was being watched and measured. And yet, she didn't feel it mattered. She no longer allowed herself to carry the weight of false perspective. The speakers played the recording of the night song and really it was beautiful. This improbable outpost, the city that belonged to her and all her kind.

The people that she passed on the street were steeped in their own mysteries—it wasn't only her who had been consumed by an omnipresent questioning—traveling past her, hands in their pockets, eyes fixed ahead on the shimmering folds of their own unique clouds, hearing the voice of private angels. Music thumped from an old-world discotheque, a small crowd of smokers hanging out front, blowing blue smoke upward, their glistening faces scooping at the fresh air and trading it for fire.

A pair of matrons appeared before her at the border with the First District. She gave her name and told them she had a delivery for Jovis. They clicked and hissed and ran her name against the files they contained behind the porce-lain smiles before letting her pass.

And when she arrived at the property Jovis called his own, Milo was waiting for her.

Once he had led her to the tropic garden at the center of the mansion, she asked him, "did you know who I was the other night when we met?"

Milo's gaze was focused loosely on the lush green canopy of faux-papaya leaves.

"After the parts of me were transferred I floated in the nothing without a body to call home. When Jovis formed me as his lackey I thought that's all I was—a duty-bound lieutenant, an automation, little more than a stone. With the outages I began to receive glimpses of who I'd been before, disconnected impressions of a dual life, two streams that carried me to this city. It was only when I came across your articles that the name Milo returned to my tongue. And it was only when Jovis told me to expect a writer named December that I realized who had written them, and only when I heard your name that some specificity of who that portion of me had been was really clear to me. I must admit I was not ready to see you yet. It felt as though I had just been with you in the natatorium in Mirror Bay, and I must admit that with a part of me I hated you."

"You have every right. I lied to you."

"Children lie. Adults commit to ideas they don't under-stand. This process is essential to the human project of bringing things into existence that did not exist before. Cities and countries are made of lies, and yet here we are, making them true."

"That makes us bankrupt, don't you think?"

"It makes us people," Milo said.

December allowed the glossy, dark frond of a parlor

palm to graze her cheek as she waded through the garden. The manuscript had been deposited on a potting bench. Milo had been tending to the imitation soil of an annual flower. Now he watched her.

"Is it true that you contain multiple lives?" she asked him.

He righted himself and dusted off his hands.

"There is a part of me that is much older than Milo ever got to be, but his name is lost. This part of me was born here. I inhabited the evernight long before there was any city here. Its builders, Jovis one of them, killed everyone I knew. They took our resource, the great tree at the center of the city that powers the factory and the lights. With this part of me I want all of you to leave, to go back to where you came from. But with this voice in me I speak to Milo, too, and it confuses me. I contain the colonizer and colonized. I can't rightly expel the part of me I know best, who sought to come here for a new life, to escape the violence. The human impulse to cross borders, to search for more favorable pastures is true, even when the lines that divide us are not."

December considered this, understanding that the meeting was by now happening, that by now there'd be someone looking for her, tracking her, searching the matrons' records. All the same, this was the conversation she wished to be in, speaking with the only person she felt could really understand all that she had been.

"Do you think we chose this? Communally I mean. I mean we must have dreamed this place and willed it into being. More of us than those who didn't want it, and thus it came to be."

"Do you mean the city or do you mean the war?" he asked.

"If what Jovis said is true, that the two are linked, then I suppose my answer's both."

For the first time, December saw him smile.

"You have the curiosity of a splintered mind," he said. "I don't have the answer but the question's good."

"I'm sorry that I interrupted your adventure. I remember Milo had dreams of sailing the open ocean."

"This house is no place for your atonement. Besides, I've learned that I contain within me the adventure that I sought, just as you have given me the very future that you stole."

"I wish that I could stay here and speak with you for all the time that we have left."

"But that's not why you came here."

"No," said December. "It's not."

By now, the boy who was Milo and something more had made his way to the potting table where December's manuscript lay.

"You have come to ask a favor."

"Yes," she said, "and it's one that might put you in danger."

"I'm listening," he said.

"The other night when I met with Jovis, I noticed that he asked you to slate something for print. Am I correct in assuming that means the press is here?"

Milo nodded.

"That stack of paper there is my final story, the last thing Jovis would want me to write."

"Do you think of it as his undoing?"

"If I'm lucky it'll play a part."

"And you'd like for me to print it for you in the *Sun*."

December nodded.

Milo picked up the stack and fanned the pages.

"This will take a lot of pulp. And it will mark you as a traitor. Then what will you do?"

"Well here I have another favor to ask. The other night Jovis mentioned the status of the Sun Country. I took that to mean he's been making visits of his own."

"Yes, he has."

"Is there a transfer machine in this house?"

"There is."

"Then I'd like you to send me home."

"What if I say no to both your queries?"

"I'll leave the pages at the carousel and walk into the night."

"Very good," he said.

Milo concealed December's story in his quarters with the promise that he would find an opportune time to print it. Then he led her to the mansion's upper floor. In a quiet room, with hardwood floors, there stood the chair she recognized, next to the squat machine.

"There is a container here where Jovis keeps his memories. His own private stock. There's a child inside him too. I've seen it. In a way, he's never grown."

"The play of children isn't always innocent."

"Depends upon the toys they have at hand."

December settled into the chair and Milo took up his position next to her, powering the machine and lifting the long, tensile needle from its hook.

"Thank you for doing this," said December.

"I'm only returning the favor," he said and lit a melancholy smile.

"Milo, I think we'd have been friends."

"December V., we are."

He conducted the transfer smoothly. Into the quiet barren, she fell.

# TWENTY

WITHOUT SUN or moon or stars to go by, without the night song and the faux-pulse of a simulated heart, without the body or the city that contained it, it was hard to measure time. All December knew was that enough of her remained to see the nothing, to float in the nothing, and to count the nothing, nothing nothing.

Until the pain came, rising in her like a flood. A liquid electricity that sparked and crackled and burned in every vein and capillary and bundle of nerves, a solution of incandescent salt, every particle of which she could feel. *Buzzing*.

The capsule in which December eventually woke was tight against her shoulders and it was tall. It reclined at an angle—this last detail she was able to interpret, thanks to a force to which she had become unaccustomed. The way the weight of a body organized itself against a physical object, itself a physical object, privy to the Sun Country's oldest rule.

The first sound she heard was the hiss of the capsule's lid opening and then its echo. The light in her corner of the vast chamber was dim. Greenish. The corneas quickly adapted to the shadows. When she sat up, she felt something long and slender slide out of the back of her neck. It didn't hurt. The pain in her extremities had also faded.

She looked around her. In the dim light she could see row after row of other capsules. There were thousands of them. Poised at an interval, every ten or so capsules, were the machines. Slightly updated, smaller, but principally the same. Squat, flat-faced, computer-like devices with dials and buttons and tanks with little paddles.

She flexed her hands and looked at them in the wan light. Yes, these hands belonged to her, but she didn't recognize them. They were knobby, thickly veined, strong-looking. The arms, too. She rubbed them and felt the tiny hairs. The sensation was outstanding, to touch and be touched, even by her own hand. Living tissue, thrumming with corporeal life. December leaned forward, almost too much. She nearly tripped stepping out of the capsule, her equilibrium challenged by the sudden movement.

A low hum emanated from somewhere in the room, somewhere close. She found the source. A fat generator in the corner of the room, sprouting ten thick cables, like exposed tree roots, one running into the back of each of the machines in her section. The green hue of its diodes providing this section of the chamber's only tinge, glinting off the other capsules.

December took her first steps. For the first time since leaving Mirror Bay for Pluto City, she felt the distribution of her body's weight onto each of her two feet. She looked down and appraised them. The feet were big, too. Contained by military boots. She felt the hard concrete beneath them. She wiggled her toes and felt them slide against one another. She ran a tongue over the teeth in her mouth. How big, how slippery.

Far away in the distance she saw another light source. She walked toward it, footsteps echoing in the cavernous room, passing capsule after capsule. They looked like seed pods, their carapaces closed tight.

So they did exist, giving credence to the lumens' story of remilitarization. And something more, too. A collective will, pushing forth, reaching for sun. The capacity for violence, yes, and the capacity for life.

When she reached the elevator door she pressed the yellow-lit button. A deep, thrumming sound came into the room and then the doors slid open. The light was bright. She stepped inside. As the compartment whooshed upward, she tried to scrutinize her reflection in the burnished steel walls, but found only a vague outline. It could be any body.

When the car reached its terminus and the doors opened, she found herself presented with a tiny anteroom. Another small door before her. She stepped off the elevator and listened.

She was struck by a sense of certainty that beyond this door, beyond this small room which now contained her in her new container, there was an outside, a real world with a sun, a moon, and stars, and beneath it hills and grass and other buildings, with shops inside them, and restaurants and roads and people, so many people, with the dramas, with the tragedies and comedies that connected them, and maybe even still war, with the shooting and the shelling, the common act of strafed amusement parks and a want for peace and a want for love, and hunger, and romance, and the living and the killing. A world she craved.

December leaned against the metal door and, slowly, it opened.

She was nearly blinded. Nearly knocked back down the stairs. For above there were frosted skylights, pouring full, gushing waterfalls of sunlight into what she recognized as a laboratory. From where she stood, eyes adjusting, feeling the change in temperature from the subterranean bunker, she could see the hallmarks of a high-tech facility. Stainless steel shelves, white floors, white walls. There were three of the machines she recognized from Mirror Bay, positioned with their backs along one wall. There were signs of damage everywhere.

What caught December's eyes first were the bodies, what was left of them. Six distinct skeletons laid in violent positions on the hard, white-tile flooring. While their clothing remained intact, the muscle, fat, and tissue had decomposed, leaving skinny postures of a death that was now antique. The blood that had been spilled from them, some time ago now, was a deep, flaking brown-black, left in smudges. Shoe-prints, too, of those who had walked away from the madness that had occurred, and the tiny bloody imprints left by small animals who had once upon a time feasted on the remains. There was no smell now. No smell at all in a room that at one time, December felt, could have been considered antiseptic.

The machines had endured the same treatment as the bodies on the floor, beaten and destroyed. They were in pieces. Their parts laid out on the floor. On the same wall, in the same blood from the floor: a cross. The mark of an old religion.

She stepped into the room. The door, which had been concealed behind a shelving unit holding glass equipment, closed silently behind her. Across the big, low-ceilinged room was what had once been a thick glass partition. Beyond this, the server racks. A little city of its own, arranged in towers, with what looked like streets laid out between them. The servers, too, were destroyed. Exposed motherboards, a dull green in the low lights, their chips and circuitry, and the little wires, exposed like the innards of skull after skull, shards of black plastic scattered on the floor beneath them, cracked open and all gathering layers of dust.

Everything here that had once lived had died some time ago, had met a brutal end, and now laid bare and innocent, like bookmarks in an old chapter of a book that nobody read anymore, written in the language of revenge.

December kept looking at the bodies, the piles of bone and leathery tissue. A sharp thought poked at her, rising in the blood. Could any of these have been her body? No. None of them were small enough. But hers had broken down, just as these did. Maybe it was in the sea, maybe it was buried underneath the ground or left on its unforgiving surface to be scavenged by the hungry. But it had met the same end as these.

She wanted to know the stories they once contained, what they had carried. And she wanted to ask of them: if you're dead now, and if the machines are all dead, and nothing here powers them, then what's supporting Pluto City? What powered it? Milo had spoken of a tree, yes, but then again if the servers were destroyed, what had stored the essences of the people there? Of Mona, Porsche, Szewski, every citizen, and who she had been? And what of the homes they went back to at the end of their shifts? If not from here, then from where did the night song play?

Could it be then that Pluto City was actual? A living, breathing place like this one? She looked again to the broken server racks, the skeletons of infrastructure. The evidence of incursion. The dust. She felt as though she was standing in a crypt or a mausoleum. Was it here that she belonged? Was she too dead, in all of the important ways?

Looking at the remains, she thought of all the lives interrupted, their courses so irrevocably changed. How does one move along a path that had been destroyed, that was surrounded on all sides by such destruction?

December felt then the emergence of two paths before her. She knew how to work the machine in the chamber in which she had awoken. She could return to what was left of the city, to the life that she knew best. The other path led outward, out into the world that had been the reason those people in Pluto City chose to flee. What if the violence here, that she too escaped, still remained? The choice came easily. She moved out of the crypt. No, with the dead she did not belong.

Connected to the lab by a fortified hallway was a private residence. She found an expansive kitchen. Above, a vaulted ceiling with exposed beams and skylights free of any glass. The window behind the sink was really just a hole left in the wall, a thick sheet of plastic, stapled to the exposed two-by-fours, a staple missing, allowing an edge to crinkle and flap in the light breeze that the outside held, pushing inward. This was the room's only sound, that corner of flapping plastic.

The warped hardwood floors had been sanded and never finished, what rainfall made it through the open skylights allowed to drip and drop onto the lengths of graying lumber. Tools had been left on the ground and on the countertops. A circular saw next to a plywood door. A hammer and a small tin of nails next to the staple-gun, next to the sink. A drill battery left to charge, no energy running to it now. Pints of varnish. A bucket full of rags and sanding tools. All of it gathering dust.

The implements sat as though the workers that had used them had planned to come back to them the next day.

A day that never came. As though the reason for their work had disappeared, or maybe they had.

December found a vague reflection of her new container in the stainless steel of the refrigerator door. She was not wearing the body of an older self, a little girl grown up, but instead the body of a man. She lifted the hands in front of her face once more and looked at the creases in his palms, in her palms. They called them life lines, once upon a time. She opened the refrigerator door, an act once so familiar. Inside it was empty, apart from a single egg, the shell gone yellowish.

She moved from room to room, looking in on the left-overs of a life interrupted. A bedroom with a wooden frame and no mattress, the lacquer on the posts flecking away. Dust settling on a small hutch. Rolled-up carpets in an otherwise empty room that reminded her of the body bags she'd seen in Gracehaven as a child. A library with empty shelves and a half-constructed fireplace, and another window with the thick plastic stapled in place, waiting for the glass that never came.

To see demonstration after demonstration of the passage of time, to see it displayed before her in such fine detail, somehow heartened her. It placed her in time, in a continuum of corporeal elements, in a process of life and decomposition that in Pluto City had only just begun. She wondered, then, for the first time since arriving—how long had she been gone from this place, this place of the sun, this place of the living? And where was she in relation to any thing or any place that she recognized? Even if she found a calendar left behind on the wall of an office, she wouldn't know how long ago the page had been flipped.

December stopped in the kitchen once more. She

checked the cupboards for supplies, for food and water, opening the old wooden doors to find them empty. And then another question came: this container, this body that was now hers, was it organic? Or was it technic? What sustenance did it require? She recalled the swatch of tissue in her father's arm, that he would peel back to show the clients, the people who would embark on the journey inward, that he used to prove to them they'd have a place here when they emerged. She pulled at the tissue in her own arm and found no seams. In one of the drawers she found a knife. She held it to the skin of her forearm, pressing lightly, feeling a little tinge of pain. Then she withdrew it. This, now, was an answer she didn't want to have. She would walk into the world. If she became thirsty, she would know. If she became hungry, she would know. She stuck the knife in the belt loop of the trousers and headed for the door.

AND THERE IT WAS, the sun above her in a blue sky. She stood for a moment and allowed the pure heat to wash over her. There was a world after all.

The compound had been constructed on a hillock and was surrounded by a short defensive wall, constructed of the same material as the great wall protecting Mirror Bay. Stacked railroad ties, dark with creosote. She could smell them from where she stood, the rich and oily petroleum hue, could smell too on the wan breeze the scent of seawater. Of salt, of drying kelp, and the roiling cycle of birth and decomposing creatures. She could hear the faint sound of seagulls, of motors, too.

There was a breach in the defensive wall, a point at which the wooden railroad ties, dark like bars of chocolate, had been blown away. She chose this as her exit and walked into the world.

Already what had come before was beginning to wash away, to lose its shape as does a vivid dream on waking. The conversation she had had with Jovis felt so far away, now. The contours of his speech, the details of their false agreement, the importance of her writing, all of it as graspable as a necklace made of antimatter. Milo, though, remained with her. He glimmered like a coin at the bottom of a fountain, catching what sunlight pierced the small volume of water between them. All of Pluto City felt this way. Submerged. Giving way now to the vista that surrounded her, the acres of golden rolling hills, decorated by the occasional boulder, and the wild, branching oaks, a future here, what could be.

December followed the scent of the sea, the sound of the gulls and of the motors. Perhaps the war she had run from was still on, and she was walking toward her death. Perhaps the war had really never happened, her time in Mirror Bay and in Gracehaven just a detail of her time in Pluto City. All she could see before her was a thick bank of grey-white fog.

The sense of recognition she felt when the great wall emerged arrested her and stopped her movement. She recognized the low hills around her, as though they had been photographed in her head, but from a different angle. The three stacks of the power plant. On the other side of the wall was the town of Mirror Bay. December could hear the low susurrus of a place alive.

She forced herself to look upon the wall. To focus on it. Unlike the defensive wall that contained the compound, there was no great breach. The wall here was intact. She scanned it and found no obvious point of entry aside from the guard tower, where she spotted tiny signs of movement. She could see the outline of a soldier in uniform.

If she chose to, she could turn back now and walk into the wide world, into all its mysteries. But the town below, as it always had, pulled at her. She mustered her spirit and proceeded forth, walking slowly, so as not to raise suspicion, so as not to give the impression of attack.

When she last saw a soldier, she was in Gracehaven. A lifetime ago, it seemed. The soldiers had been much taller then. She realized, quickly, they must have seemed so tall because she had been so little. She was ten or eleven at the time. The one that stepped out of the guard tower now, through a door on the ground floor, wore a camouflaged fatigue she could not place. It was not the green and brown, pixelated pattern of the Theo forces—those in the regular company, who stooped to wearing designating material— nor was it the gray and blue of the Numeral forces. Instead, the uniform was all one color, a lightish blue. He wore no patches. His skin was pale. He was her height. He carried a rifle, barrel pointed lazily at the ground. Surprisingly, he smiled.

"Where in the hell did you blow in from?" he said, with good humor in his voice.

December was relieved by the absence of animosity in the soldier's bearing, which left her energy to consider the question he had asked. Yet she struggled to find the words. The soldier waited, as though he had all the time.

"That's hard for me to answer," she said, the voice sounding too deep to recognize as her own. "I've just come from someplace very far away."

"I understand," he said. "We're all a little bit that way. You got your papers?"

Instinctively she patted her pockets. She felt nothing of the sort.

"No," she said. "I don't."

"Fair enough," he said. "Let me just get a scan of your chip."

December stood in place, unsure what he meant.

"Come on over, brother. I don't mean you any harm."

The soldier lifted his hands off the body of the rifle, letting it dangle on the strap.

"You look a little gun shy. Where'd you fight?" he said.

"I wasn't in the war," she said.

"Oh sure you were. That's one thing none of us escaped."

Still, she didn't move.

"Fine then, I'll come to you," he said. "But don't get skittish, okay? I come in peace, but this thing does shoot."

The soldier approached her and, as he did, pulled a slender device from a velcro pouch on his flak jacket. The sound was one she had not heard in ages. Hearing it oddly soothed her.

"Lift up your arms, alright."

December felt numb. The experience of emerging in the Sun Country once more, of sensing Mirror Bay, as though nothing had happened, was echoing across her mind in waves, subduing her thoughts and movements. The soldier waved the scanner over her body, over her head, and neck, and arms, then down her chest and the inside and outside of her legs.

The scanner beeped and he read the little pixelated screen. He whistled.

"Jimmy Christ, I haven't seen this model in a while. This is an early one. A carrier. Where'd you say you've been?"

"Model of what?" she asked.

"One of the early technics. A nice one. They only made a few. Boy you sure you didn't fight? This thing you're in's a killer, hardly needs any tuneups at all. If you ever think of selling, I know a guy. There are models better suited for civilian life, if that's your plan."

"No, I..." December stumbled over her words, taking in the news. The body she was in was technic after all. Artificial. Just like her father's.

"What brings you to Mirror Bay?"

"I used to live here, in a house on Chief Street."

"Oh, yeah? And when was that?" he asked. For the first time, a sliver of disbelief tinged his voice.

"I don't know, that must have been. Oh, I don't know," she racked her brain. "2058, I think. Maybe '59. Wait, what year is it?"

"Man, that was a fucked year around these parts. Today is March 18th, 2078. You picked a good time to come back."

"Twenty years," December murmured. "Twenty years I've been gone."

Just then, a series of pops and explosions let out, somewhere on the Mirror Bay side of the wall. December flinched, an old instinct compelling her to find a place to shelter.

The soldier laughed, good natured and open, and shook his head.

"Assholes," he said.

"What was that?"

"Every month it seems some drunks get ahold of the fireworks."

"Is it safe here?"

"Pretty much," he said.

"So the war is over?"

"I wouldn't go that far," he smiled. "No, there's still shit popping off here and there. But nobody wants to fuck up the party town. People come here to blow off some steam. Find some comfort, if you know what I mean. You know, you look a little stressed. You could probably use some, too."

"Oh," she said.

"Come on in, let's get your papers."

He turned his back on her and walked toward the guard shack. He noticed she didn't follow.

"Unless you want to stay out here. Nobody's forcing you," he said.

December found she wanted nothing more than to see the other side of the wall. She followed him into the guard shack, where he slid around to a little desk, where a computer—old looking—sat, plugged into a socket in the wall.

"Do you have any weapons?" he said.

"No, I..."

"It's okay if you do. We just need to register them. You can pick them up whenever you leave."

"I do have a knife," she said, remembering the kitchen knife she'd stuck in her waist line. She pulled it out, presenting it to the soldier in an open palm.

The soldier laughed.

"That you can keep," he said. "In case you run into a good steak. Not that you need it. I'm serious about the body. If you think of selling you come back and let me know."

The soldier lifted a digital camera to his eye, squinting in the viewfinder.

"Smile, if that's your thing."

He didn't wait but a moment before the flash went off.

"What's your name?" he asked. "First and last."

"December. December Valence," she said.

"Never heard that one before. Sorta sounds like a woman's name, don't you think?"

"I was living in Pluto City," said December, as though some gate in her had opened. "That's where I was."

"Is that that commune out there, outside Three Notches?"

December realized that to mention anything about the lumens' plan to train up the citizens of Pluto City as a fighting force, to put them into the bodies in the capsules like her own, to push them forth and reignite the war, would only raise the soldier's hackles. She could imagine the story rippling outward, giving cause for further armament, bringing about the very condition Jovis desired.

"No," she said. "It's in the evernight, far from here, in a place where there isn't any light. There's a city there, and people living in it. Good people, trying to make a life. I tried to help, the only way I knew how."

"Mhmm."

The soldier was focused on the screen of his computer, clicking and typing. His window of curiosity had shut. She heard the inner workings of a printer, somewhere beneath the desk. He handed her a sheet of paper.

"Keep this on you," he said. "You have thirty days. If you secure employment in that time, update your status with City Hall. If you haven't and you haven't gotten into any serious trouble, you can likely get your pass renewed."

"Oh, thanks," she said, taking it, feeling the thickness of the paper in her hands. Real paper, Sun Country pulp, so different from what she held, from what she'd bled on in Pluto City. The sensation was grand.

"Can I be honest with you, Valence?" said the soldier.

"Go on," December said.

"Wherever you've been, we've all been there. Nobody's really gonna want to hear your war stories, whatever it was you did," he said. "Just get you some rest. Make a little stop at the Sable Inn. You won't be sorry."

And he winked at her, and lifted his arm toward the door.

"On behalf of the territorial guard of the California Central Division, welcome back to Mirror Bay. You're free to go about your business."

December stepped out of the guard shack and felt again the soft earth beneath her feet. From where she stood, she could see the town below, nestled against the coastline. The foggy harbor. Ships gently tipping in the slow tide. The little homes. The jewel and terror of her upbringing. The town of Mirror Bay. All at once she felt the impulse to run, not toward it but away. Her breaths came sharply. A sudden panic. The feeling charged at her but she held her ground.

Is this not what she wanted? To return to the Sun Country and pick up the life that she had left off? Is this not what she hoped to find? But she wasn't any more what she had been—she wasn't that little girl who had left Mirror Bay, guilty and afraid. Of course she wasn't. But to see it now, laid out before her in all its lazy grandeur confirmed to her that it had happened: the war and the transferring, the interruption of so many futures, the part she played in that. Of course it had.

———

THE TOWN FELT SMALLER than it had to her as a child. The homes not as tall, the streets narrower. At the same time, it felt larger for what she knew it was connected to, how it stretched into her, and beyond, to the rest of the Sun Country and the greater world. A place connected to all others by the threads of those who had come here, who had left, who were yet to arrive. The stories they carried within them, each of us, the legacy of what had happened, generation to generation, year to year, marching irreparably toward a multiplicity of present moments. This moment only one of them, and yet containing pieces of every moment before, and every moment to come, like seeds laid between the folds of a wet cloth and left to germinate, the stock that bore them long since buried, returned to soil, the roots of the next, waking in the husk. She was reminded of a feeling she had had in Pluto City, of being moored on a small vessel, far away from any land. A feeling of essential disconnection that here was gone. Knowing that the land beneath her feet was connected to yet more land, lapped at by the grand Pacific Ocean, intoxicated her with possibility.

Although it had been some two decades since she last walked on Chief Street, then in the body of a child with bad headaches, she knew the way, the memory of the route embedded in her somewhere. December found the house that she and August had lived in without trying very hard. The streets here were quiet. Though there were a few motor vehicles parked along the sidewalks, none were moving. Their tires looked old and bald. The yard of the house on Chief Street was overgrown. The house, like the rest of the houses, had not received any new coats of paint, it seemed, since she had been here last. So the blue that she had associated with it had run to gray and the wooden walls looked shriveled and choked. She stood outside the rusted metal gate.

In an upstairs window of the house, she noticed the face of a young girl. To find something as still as she was, who looked to be just as alive, startled her. For a moment, the two looked at one another. December waved. The girl did not wave back. The girl merely stood and leveled her gaze onto December from the second-story window. The girl looked to be ten or eleven years old and was dressed as one might before going to bed, in spite of the daylight fighting valiantly through the thick fog. December decided she would approach the house, and knock, and try to speak with her. The steps creaked, each of them, as did the wooden deck as the boots carried her to the old, familiar door. December knocked and waited. Then she knocked again. She saw the reflection of the new face, now hers, and understood then what the girl had seen. A strange man standing on the street, watching her, unsmiling. Ultimately she was unsurprised when the girl never came, never opened the door to greet her. The little girl had chosen safety. This she understood.

December peered into the windows, savoring what details she could gather through the panes, which had acquired a thick layer of gray material, particles of sea air, salt, and grime. She could see into the living room, where the same old mantle stood, at its feet the thick oblong, woven rug, and into the kitchen, where she recognized a corner of the granite countertop and the center island. The lights were off and she didn't see the girl or the movement of anybody else, just an empty-looking place that had once contained her. She had laid on her back on that rug once, on her last night here. On the mantle there had been candles, flickering in the cold draft. The rain had run down these very windows. And in the kitchen she had eaten meals, her father watching her, chewing nothing for himself. It was another life, for other people, who had vanished and become something else.

December was tired, soul-deep. In a sense she had accomplished her goal; she had proven to herself that after all she had a spirit; there was a core to her and it was solid. Through three incarnations, three phases, she had attained a certain continuity. That she made it here, that she carried her memories with her still, was proof enough. But she felt transient. She felt as though all she had ever been was on the move. From Gracehaven, here. For twenty years, in Pluto City. That would make her thirty-two or thirty-three years of age. An age she never thought she'd reach. There was a sense of victory here, tingling into her fingertips. And yet, she felt as though she was still missing something. That there were still holes in her somewhere.

She knocked on the door once more, hoping to prove that she was not what she appeared to be. Another soldier, another vagrant, another father expressing false claims to the power of protection. But the girl she had seen in the window never came. Eventually, December turned away from the house on Chief Street and allowed the memory in her muscles to carry her along the old route, down Luzon. She walked among the houses she had once named. Pilar, Marvin, Becky, Mother. Their paint was faded now, but she still recognized them. She wondered at how she had chosen the names. From where had they originated? She felt a tenderness toward her former self, so innocent then, in spite of what had happened in the natatorium.

The old route carried her toward Mirror Bay's downtown. As she neared it, she could hear music. Voices, conversations, ringing bells, and over this a sort of violin, waving and careening off the waning light. The temperature was changing. The sun had begun its descent. She could detect a slight shift in the atmosphere, an abeyance in the clouds. It became cooler. She felt a chill. She felt suddenly very lonely as she turned left onto Main Street and beheld what the town had become.

On either side of the street, built atop the sidewalks and jutting into the center of the lane were the stalls of a carnival. Brightly painted. Reds, yellows. Sharp blues. Adult men and women stood in ones and twos, some in groups, some dressed in army fatigues, others in finery. Suits and dresses. A couple, man and woman, looked to be wearing western costumes from the old Sun Country, far back, what it used to be: wide-legged jeans and oversized denim coats. Sneakers. A felt hat. They lobbed heavy balls at a stack of wooden bottles. Prizes of plush toys hung on steel grating, stood tall. BB guns let off small, concentrated puffs of air as two military men shot at paper cutouts. Small intervals between the amusements revealed darkened doors. Out of one of them stumbled three men, about her age, drunken, eyes adjusting to the light. Their faces caught in a happy, unfeeling rictus. December looked at the ground. It was strewn heavily with straw, varied by bits of torn newspaper. Some large enough to display legible text.

She walked between the stalls, feeling at once as though she were ten again, frequenting the amusement park in Gracehaven, where her father worked then. She remembered one fateful day, when he had picked her up from school early. A boy had been shot that day, by another boy, during recess in the gym. She had seen it happen. She had heard it. The pops had been loud. The boy was struck several times. The force of the rounds had knocked him over. He had fallen on his back. He kept trying to get up, but his body understood something he didn't yet. August had come to pick her up. She was glad to have a parent. At least one. She rode in the backseat. August had a mustache then and he wore the shabby clown's outfit that he donned on days when he acted in the plays. He kept looking at her in the rearview. His eyes were soft. This was before the University, before the transfers, when he still worked at the amusement park, when his body was still his own.

"There's someone I want you to meet," he said, smiling softly.

It was autumn. The leaves that grew on the trees in the park were drying and falling wonderfully. She held his hand and, as they walked through the amusement park, she hunted down the best and crunchiest leaves to step on. At the time, she thought she knew who she was going to finally meet. As December remembered the day now, her eyes welled with tears. This memory had been locked in her, deep in her, and feeling it now forced her toward one of the darkened intervals between the stalls.

Holding her father's hand that day, she had brimmed with an excitement. In her mind, she was going to meet her mother. The woman she had never known. Details of her existence had been scant ever since she had grown old enough to ask about her. August had always changed the subject, preferring to conceal what he knew. What she, this day, would learn.

He took her toward one of the oldest buildings in the park, past the Ferris wheel that hadn't run since it was damaged by the strafing fire of an airship. He guided her through a set of doors that in all of her explorations of the park, she had never entered. Inside was a house of mirrors. The air was cool. The lights were dim and as he led her through the confusing, winding halls, the walls of which obscured and flattened and extended her reflection, she wondered idly why her mother was waiting here, of all places, to meet her, to finally hold her in her arms.

In the center of the house of mirrors was a tall, domed room. Every facet of the walls and faraway ceiling were covered by smaller pieces of mirror so that when you looked up, you saw yourself refracted, doubled, tripled.

"Now, December," said August, kneeling to settle his eyes onto hers. "I know that life here has become very complicated. And you're the toughest girl who ever was. But I wanted to show you this. Look around you, and don't forget. No matter where you go in life, no matter how alone you feel, you will always have your many selves around you. Past yous and the yous of the future will always be there to watch over you, and in kind you'll be watching over them. Look up. Look up. Do you see? Isn't she beautiful? Isn't she strong?"

He was pointing up at the domed ceiling of the center of the house of mirrors but she kept her eyes on him.

"December," he said again. "Look up."

"Where is she?" said December.

August didn't understand.

"I thought I was going to meet my mom," she finally said.

And in an instant she could tell she crushed him, at least a little part of his big self. Perhaps, December figured now, this was when he realized he didn't have very much for her. That he couldn't account for what she'd lost.

"Why don't you ever talk about her? Why don't I ever get to see her?" December said.

And it was there in the house of mirrors that August told her.

"December. I never knew your mom," he said, as though he had decided this was as good a time as any. "You showed up at the park one night, barely old enough to walk. You must have seen the lights and followed them. You were covered in soot. You didn't have anywhere to go and you were hungry. I looked and looked for anybody who could claim you, but this was a very difficult time in the city, when most of the bombing happened. A lot of people died. Your mother may have been one of them we lost."

Standing here in Mirror Bay now, hidden between a basketball hoop and a roller ball game, the rhythmic sound of the wooden balls sliding up the ramp, and of the rubber balls bouncing against a metal rim, she could feel how bereft she'd been hearing her father tell her that there was no mother to be found. That he was not actually her father, that they'd shared no blood. It was the first time in her young life that she had been so angry, that she had felt as though her life was made of lies.

A trilling, metallic, artificial song spewed out of a set of speakers attached to the basketball game. Someone must have won. She had the impulse to run, to scream. She forced herself to walk slowly and concertedly away from the carnival. Once she had put some distance between her and the crowd, she let it out. A deep, bony howl. She made her hands into fists and she stamped and screamed again, with such force that her throat began to hurt, as though it were composed of sensitive tissue. The little, scratching pain distracted her for a moment, making her wonder if perhaps the body wasn't artificial after all. Maybe the soldier had been wrong. Maybe all of them had been wrong, all the people who had told her with such confidence what her life meant, what was most important to believe.

She reached the land's terminus, where sea met craggy cliff. The boats tilted, to and fro, in the harbor. The seagulls gathered on light posts and on the docks' weathered banisters, gathering their warmth for the coming night. In the distance, the clouds relented, exposing a band of infinite horizon, where the sun, that beautiful, reddened orb dipped toward the sea.

What would she have done with her life here had she not left it for Pluto City? What if she had stayed in Gracehaven or remained here in Mirror Bay? What would have become of that December? She tried to remember her childhood desires. Nothing came to mind but the will to escape. She had wanted to escape her headaches; she had wanted to escape the thrumming drumbeat of the war; she had wanted to impress her only friend, her father, and through this escape the smallness she had felt then, the powerlessness meted out to the young and little-bodied. She felt as though she had only been responding to external stimuli, her life contingent on the greater currents of a world so much larger, and older, and more powerful than she could fully grasp. She understood, now, that her father had been, too. Truly, what did anybody really choose? Even when you did marshal your resources around a particular objective—and let's say you did it, let's say you got where you wanted to go —the world changed again by the time you got there, presenting new needs, a new current to navigate with or against. So what then was the value of your soul, your spirit, that which was contained by whichever body held you, if in fact it was merely another ripple in a vast and open ocean that swallowed up all individual causality?

December walked along a path between the thick-fingered ice plant. She had for so long allowed herself to be caught up in and consumed by a paradigm that cared nothing for her. Suffocated by the weight of history, of history's constant interrogation. She remembered clearly now the little girl she had once been. The little girl who missed her mom, this woman she had never met, who for her represented some fundamental guidance that she had to live without. Her adopted father was her hero for a time but he forsook her. She had felt that both her parents had. She could no longer blame them for failing like every parent before them to protect their children from the world. Because the world had come for all of us, shattering the home we had, orphaning us from the kind of life that we would ever recognize.

December reached the natatorium. The peaked chunk of concrete, squat and solid. Steam—or was it smoke?—rose from a vent fan in the roof, wafting over the cross that had been affixed to its center peak like a mast. This, the birthplace of a second her.

She walked past it. She did not enter. She put it behind her; she chose not to relive what had transpired there. She had already been, in one way or another, living in a story that did not belong to her, that she decided she no longer belonged to. She found a place on the cliffside, clear of ice plant, and sat. The clouds had cleared. As the sun fell away into the sea, night came.

She knew that Pluto City had been real, that the evernight had been real, that the place she had inhabited for twenty years of her life had been as actual as anything else, this town, this sea, this body. How it had come to be, the precise origin of its refuge, she could not be sure. She knew that she was here and that everyone she had come to know was someplace close. It occurred to her that the self was only a temporary refuge, delicate and impermanent as a drop of dew. The feeling that she had of being moored, far away from any land or any person, she let it fall. It didn't matter where she was or what contained her. This was a feeling she had chosen because she was in pain. She imagined this feeling as physical, as though it was a stone she could hold in her hand, and she tossed it into the sea. She was alive and curious. She could improvise and love. This was the value of a soul.

And the stars stretched out above her, glimmering in their appointed homes. She could hear them. She listened to their song.

## ACKNOWLEDGMENTS

Thanks to:

The cities of Los Angeles, Portland, Seattle, Santa Cruz, and Brooklyn. To the towns of Grass Valley and Morro Bay. To the Southwest Chief.

Thank you to all the friends who have supported me throughout the process of making this book. Thanks to Francis and to Yoakum.

To the Group—Aatif, Rachel, Alex, Dom, and Noah—who read countless iterations of the manuscript and all its pieces. Your generosity and incisiveness is ever humbling.

To my teachers, Ron, Liska, Chris, Lou. Especially Mr. Cartan, the aficionado.

Thank you to Debi and Ezra. Your love and support is ever felt. Mom, you especially, for teaching me the love of reading.

Finally and foremost thanks to Amber, without whom this book, and my self as I know it, would not exist.

## ABOUT THE AUTHOR

Jon H. Eddy was born in Sacramento, California and grew up in the foothills of the Sierra Nevada Mountains. His short fiction has appeared in the Hoxie Gorge Review and Spectrum Literary Journal, and has been performed at Lit Crawl Los Angeles and as part of the New Short Fiction Series. *Into the Quiet Barren* is his first novel.